THE RIBBONS IN THE TREES

THE OKRITH NOVELLAS
BOOK SIX

A.K. MULFORD

Paperback: 978-1-923184-13-8

Ebook: 978-1-923184-12-1

Cover by MiblArt

Map by Holly Dunn Designs

Interior Formatting by K. Elle Morrison

NORTHERN COU
Murreneir
Brufdoran
DRUNEHAN
Vurstyn
HIGH MOUNTAIN COURT
Valtene
YEXSHIRE
SEA OF
CALLIPHO
SWIFTHILL
WESTERN
COURT
Silver
Sands
Harbor
OKRITH

N
SEA OF WETAMUIR
enport
Falhampton
ROTTED PEAK
EASTERN COURT
WYNREACH
Haastmouth
SOUTHERN COURT
Crushwold
SAXBRIDGE

CONTENT WARNINGS

This book contains themes of loss, fire, violence, war, as well as sexually explicit scenes.

Spoiler Warning

This book contains spoilers from *The High Mountain Court*

CHAPTER ONE

The wagon jostled down the rocky trail, and the red witch's arm never left her side. Emry's reassuring grip held onto Heather as if she might disappear. Sunlight danced through the speckled autumnal trees as butterflies fluttered in Heather's chest. Mother Moon, she'd really done it. The most wild and impulsive thing of her life —she'd run off with a beautiful red witch, to join a carnival no less.

The caravan trailed southward, hugging along the temperate forests in the shadow of the High Mountains. As they pulled past little villages, children ran out to watch the colorful rainbow of painted wagons. They waved and wagon drivers thumbed silver *druni* to the delighted children. Heather heard the calls of other witches up ahead, promising they would stay longer on the next trip.

Everyone wanted the *Carnivale du Fareas* to stop in their hometown. In every witch's home, they talked about the fabled carnival. Little witchlings hoped each year would be the year *Carnivale du Fareas* stopped in their village.

What if they hadn't stopped in Valtene this year . . .

Heather shook off the thought like a sudden chill. She couldn't think about "what if"s anymore. She was here. She made her choice. For the first several hours of their journey she had wanted to look back over her shoulder, but she refrained, focusing instead on the road before her.

They stopped to water the horses at midday, finding a forested strip of road to pull to the side and set up lunch. Even as the wagon slowed, Heather's heart still hammered in her chest. She'd have to actually talk to Emry now. She laughed at herself at the thought. Shouldn't that be the easiest part of all this?

As she worried her lip, she clenched her hands together in her lap. Should she be the one to speak first? What would she even say? *Hi, I've decided to leave my entire life and family to run off with you because every time I look at you my insides melt into molten ore?*

How was she supposed to move her body without looking so painfully awkward? Moon Goddess, help her! She'd never done any of this before. Her heartbeat choked her as her cheeks flamed and she sat on her hands to keep them from visibly trembling. Maybe this was all a mistake . . .

But the second Emry pulled her dappled gray mare to a halt, she dropped the horse's reins, grabbed Heather by both cheeks, and kissed her. No thinking required. No awkwardness. She kissed Heather like she'd been desperate for her kiss since the moment Heather got on the wagon.

Heather released her pinned hands and allowed her arms to circle Emry's back, delighting in the feeling of the red witch's soft lips on hers. With a single kiss, her fears were assuaged. She pressed her fingertips into Emry's muscled back and urged her closer.

Emry smiled against her mouth, breaking their kiss to rest her forehead against Heather's. Red witch magic glowed from Emry's fingertips as she lowered her hands from

Heather's cheeks. Heather thanked the Moon for the flare of witch magic and the visible sign that Emry was as overwhelmed with emotions as Heather was herself.

Heather stared breathlessly into Emry's glowing gaze. "Your eyes are the most beautiful crimson right now."

Emry's cheeks dimpled as she grinned. "And yours the most brilliant bronze."

The warm buzzing of Heather's brown witch magic tingled across her cheeks and up her fingertips.

"Only a quick one," a feminine voice barked as heavy boots crunched down the line. "Ten minutes and we'll be on the move again. We need to reach Goldrick before sunset and—"

A middle-aged woman turned the corner, wearing a tricorne hat, thin silver-streaked locks spilling from the brim. She wore a double-breasted wool coat with golden buttons and ballooning tan breeches. Heather attempted to school her expression and not gawk at the woman. She looked more like she captained a ship with a dastardly crew than a carnival witch . . . Every member of *Carnivale du Fares* looked more eccentric than the next.

The woman paused, pursing her lips at Heather and balancing her bucket of wrapped parcels on her hip. "And who might this be, Em?"

She had a strong Western Court accent, probably from the seafaring towns on the border with the Southern Court.

"Heather, this is our fearless leader, Drea Yirloana." Emry wrapped her arm around Heather's side. "Drea, this is Heather." Drea tipped the corner of her hat to Heather, and Heather nervously bobbed her head in return. "She's a brown witch from Valtene and an apothecary apprentice. She's going to be helping me run my stall."

"And how long is this Heather going to be joining us?" Drea asked Emry with a tilt of her head.

Emry glanced at Heather, her red magic flickering. "As long as she desires."

Heather's arms pimpled with gooseflesh at the sound of Emry's raspy promise.

"Two parcels, then." Drea snickered, passing Emry two bundles wrapped in cream-colored tea towels. "Ten minutes and we leave." She shook her head with a wry grin as she glanced between the two of them. "I give it a month."

Emry passed Heather the parcel, the fabric tied in a bow. Under the towel she felt something spongy, bread or pastry of some kind. Emry's pointer finger trailed down Heather's hand, and Heather pressed her lips together to keep a ridiculous smile from forming. They were here. Together.

Drea chuckled, swaggering back down the row as she mumbled to herself, "Aye, maybe two months."

Heather and Emry exchanged conspiratorial glances, and Heather wondered if Emry also took Drea's statement as a challenge. Forget two months. How about two decades? How about more? Heather daydreamed of the life unspooling before her as they unwrapped their lunches. Emry lifted a triangle of her pastry and paused, smiling.

"What?" Heather asked, unable to hide her matching grin. A thrill ran through her.

"I'm just . . ." Emry laughed, the two of them giggling at the ridiculousness of it all. "I'm just glad you're here."

Heather took a bite of her pie, the savory filling lighting up her taste buds. Emry lifted her thumb and wiped a flaky bit of pastry from the corner of Heather's mouth.

"I'm glad I'm here too," she mumbled through her mouthful of food.

They laughed together in giddy disbelief, eating their lunches as if they were children sneaking treats. Joy burst from the center of Heather's chest. She was a traveling carnival witch now.

CHAPTER TWO

As the sun fell toward the horizon, they pulled into a dusty field dotted with sparse golden grasses. Only a day's journey south, the landscape was so different from Valtene. As they traveled farther from the drizzly forests and quiet tavern towns, the terrain shifted. The leafy burnt-orange forest turned to spiky plants, scrub brush, and lean trees whose canopies billowed like chartreuse clouds along the horizon.

The lead wagon pivoted onto the open plain, twisting inward as the other wagons followed in a perfect spiral. It was a practiced dance—one Heather was more than a little interested in seeing how they'd reverse. The drivers dismounted and set about their evening routines with practiced ease. They watered and unhitched the horses and gathered them in a herd to graze as the sun set. Three shaggy black-and-gray dogs appeared from the wagons and roamed the edges of the herd.

Heather squinted at the horizon. "Do they have wolves this far south?" she murmured, more to herself than to Emry.

"Many a beast roams these parts," Emry said, waggling

her fingers like she was telling a spooky tale. But when Heather shuddered, she hastily added, "But they sense the concentration of our collective magic and steer clear. Horses have no such magic though, hence the dogs."

With that little added reassurance, Heather stood, stretching her weary arms above her head as the blood flowed back into her legs. Sitting on that hard wooden bench all day had made her sore all over. She'd used muscles she didn't know she had to keep from falling over.

Emry hopped off the open side of the driver's seat and lifted a hand up to help Heather down. Heather dropped, stumbling a step forward and bumping her chest into Emry's as her arms shot out to catch herself. Emry smiled, giving her a chaste peck on her lips as Heather's soft body slid down Emry's muscled one. When her feet touched the ground, Emry didn't immediately let her go.

Cheeks flushed, Heather lifted onto her toes and planted a returning kiss on Emry's mouth. The heated moment sent tingles from the crown of her head all the way down to her toes. Even as her heart galloped in her chest, something in her sighed too. Emry eased every other worry in her mind with the rightness she felt when they kissed.

"I think the traveling life has made you bolder. I like it." Emry's hands circled her waist, her lips grazing Heather's temple as she murmured, "I don't think I can go two minutes without kissing you."

"We nearly knocked our teeth out testing that theory on the wagon." She chuckled, thinking of those looks they gave each other the entire ride. Every time Emry had peeked at her, she'd wanted to kiss her again.

"We'll just have to settle for my arm around you," Emry said. "We'll be in Saxbridge for the entire winter season. No traveling."

Heather flashed a soft little smile. "I can't wait."

The stout blue witch with a curling black mustache passed them and laughed. "Welcome to *Carnivale du Fareas*, Heather," he said, tipping his cap to her.

She blanched, wondering how he knew her name and then remembering he was a blue witch. He must have gleaned her name from his gift of Sight.

"Ean Mallor." He offered out his hand and she shook it, stepping out of Emry's hold.

"That was some stunt you pulled with the wagon wheel, Mallor," Emry said. "You could've just said we needed to wait."

"Aye, where's the fun in that?" His eyes twinkled a swirling sapphire blue. "I just came up from the spring. The droughts hit heavy, but there's a trickle if you need to fill your skins."

"Thanks." Emry tipped her chin to him as he carried on down the curving line of wagons toward the center of the spiral. "See you at dinner."

More of the carnival witches began walking toward the center of the spiral, gathering as night descended. Heather tried to count them all—at least forty.

"We're just passing through," Emry said, glancing at Heather as she watched the campsite spring to life. "We only unpack the essentials for dinner."

Heather stared at the thin trail of smoke already rising in the center of the spiral. The savory scent of the green witches' cooking filled the air. Her mouth started salivating at the wafting aroma of tea and spices.

"Don't trust the heat now." Emry nodded to Heather's cloak. "When the sun dips below the horizon, the ground will be covered in frost."

Emry lifted her hand to Ravi and the raven jumped onto her arm. She stroked her hand down his iridescent black feathers as she swung out the perch tucked under the windowsill for travel. He hopped back onto his perch with a piercing caw.

Chuckling, Emry said, "I'll get you your dinner in a minute."

The sky filled with strange pinks and brilliant golds as the eagerest of stars started blinking to life above them. The tall, narrow trees cast long shadows across the savanna as insects buzzed and night birds sang a strange cooing song. They had only been riding for a day and already Heather felt so far from home.

As if sensing her nerves, Emry took a step forward. "There's an underground spring that breaks through just downhill from here." She pointed past the blue-and-gold wagon in front of them. "It's not wide enough to bathe in, but nice to splash some cool water on your face and fill your skin with water."

"Have you camped here before?"

"Every turn around Okrith, we stop in Galdrick." Emry lifted her arms above her head, stretching out her muscles after the long ride. A flash of skin peeked from the hem of her tunic, and Heather's heart leapt into her throat. "It's just enough outside town that we don't have any disappointed kids wondering if we're setting up shop. Nice open space for the horses, big sky views, and water nearby." Her heavy hooded gaze dropped to Heather. "It's what every traveler wants . . . well that, and someone to share it with."

Heather's stomach clenched at those slow words coming from Emry's full lips. *Someone to share it with.* And suddenly she wanted to see every corner of Okrith with Emry by her side. That calm confidence made her feel steady, even as everything around her was changing. What endless stories would she be able to one day tell?

Ravi cawed again, breaking the spell between their eyes and making Heather jolt.

"All right, I'll get you dinner," Emry jeered, glaring at him over her shoulder. "You did that on purpose," she muttered to her bird. Turning back to Heather, she gave her one more kiss on the cheek. "You get used to him."

Heather huffed, watching as Emry ambled toward the back of the midnight-and-gold wagon, the cackles of witch laughter filling the air, the intoxicating scent of green witch cooking wafting on the breeze, and the night sky speckled with glittering stars.

"I don't think I'll ever get used to this."

CHAPTER THREE

As they meandered down the spiral, Heather's pulse raced anew at the thought of meeting the famed *Carnivale du Fareas* witches. Her footsteps slowed more and more until Emry was practically dragging her along. Emry looked back over her shoulder with an arched brow of amusement. The look on her face already asked the question, and she waited patiently for Heather to answer.

"Will the others mind that I'm here?" Heather asked sheepishly.

"How do you think we all ended up here?" Emry smiled ruefully. "Some are runaways, others just have an insatiable wanderlust. The carnival numbers are constantly expanding and contracting. So no, the others most certainly won't mind."

"Okay. Good." Heather released their joined hands to wrap an arm around Emry's waist. She leaned into Emry as they walked down the spiral, red dust kicking up around their feet.

"Some witches have been a part of the carnival for generations, others only stay for a season," Emry continued. "As long as you're willing to help, we don't turn anyone away, magic or no."

Heather thought about Emry's offer from only a few days ago. Gods, it felt like a lifetime. The arm wrapped around her shoulders now felt like it had been there forever. Emry had said that she needed a brown witch to turn her exotic herbs into potions, and Heather's father had sent her off with a heaving pack of wares too. With any luck, soon she'd have a heavy bag of *druni* to send back to her family.

"Do you have any other brown witches in the carnival?" Heather wondered aloud.

"We have four," Emry replied, sliding her warm brown eyes to Heather. "Though none have grown up in an apothecary like you."

"What do they do?"

"Not all our jobs are tied to our magic." Emry waggled her fingers, conjuring her red magic into flames at their tips. A lock of Heather's copper-red hair floated up off her cloak. "I, for instance, run an exotic herb trade despite my powers of animation." Heather's hair dropped back onto her shoulder again as Emry let out a playful chuckle. "There are artists and artisans, fire dancers and acrobats, some care for the horses, others care for the children, some cook, some mend . . . we help in whatever ways we know how."

"As long as you don't ask me to be an acrobat, I will do anything else."

Emry snorted, squeezing Heather's shoulder. "No tightrope for you, got it."

They ambled into the center of the spiral as smoke curled around them. Two women loomed over a burgeoning fire while others worked in pairs, pulling benches from the back of the wagons and arranging them in an octagon around the fire. It was the same setup as the nights when the carnival had been in Valtene, except instead of patrons using the seating to watch the dancers and acrobats, the carnival witches now used it to gather for dinner.

Witchlings raced about, chasing each other between the wagons. The sight of them made Heather think of Oliver and Evelyn—her little brother and sister would've loved this. An unfamiliar ache radiated through her. She didn't know how long it would be until she saw them again.

"Everyone," Emry called to the group, their faces turning to the red witch one by one. "This is Heather. She's a brown witch from Valtene and she'll be joining us on the journey to Saxbridge."

Heather's cheeks tingled and flamed as they assessed her. She was certain beads of sweat were collecting on her top lip, but with everyone watching, she refrained from swiping it away. These witches were so unlike her coven back home. They all wore zany clothes, like nothing she'd ever seen before—beads, velvets, ribbons, feathers, lace, and gems in every possible shade—each outfit an eccentric mishmash of the stylings of all five courts.

"I know you all want to get to know her, but don't all bombard her at once, okay?" Emry added, and the group laughed in unison.

The elderly women tending the fire gave knowing glances to the children who eagerly watched Heather.

Drea took a step out of the throng and the rest of the witches made way for her. She removed her tricorne hat and bowed her head to Heather. "Welcome to the carnival, Heather."

"Welcome!" the crowd echoed after their leader.

Most of them heeded Emry's warning and turned back to their tasks.

Everyone seemed to seize the opportunity of stillness before they were to head out on the road the next morning. Two witches to Heather's right sat on their tailgates, mending patches in their clothes. A witch to her left shook out her towel and hung it on a string that was tied to the wagon behind. Three witchlings peeked at her from beyond the fire, whispering to each other.

"New arrivals always stir up excitement," Emry murmured, hooking her thumb at the children and adding, "They're harmless. Mostly."

Heather pressed her lips together, letting Emry guide her into the middle row of benches. A silver-haired witch approached them, holding two steaming mugs.

Her green eyes glowed as she asked, "Tea, dears?"

"Yasmin, meet Heather. Heather, this is Yasmin," Emry said, taking her mug as she made her introductions.

"Welcome to the carnival, Heather," Yasmin said. Heather rose to take her mug so that the stooped old witch wouldn't have to bend over. "We could always use a few more brown witches around here."

"Thank you," Heather replied more softly than she intended. She brought the warm cup to her lips, the soothing liquid coating her dry throat.

"Remind me to ask you about my hip, tomorrow," Yasmin added with a wink before shuffling back toward the fire. Her totem bag swayed with each movement, bouncing off her chest.

"Isn't one of your brown witches the carnival healer?" Heather asked. The benches filled around her as the witches gathered for dinner.

"They are, but they're not very good." Swallowing another sip of tea, Emry shook her head. "They didn't have strong enough magic to find good work as a brown witch in their hometowns. It's why a lot of the witches have joined the carnival."

Towns were filled with witches whose magic was barely an ember. Most often, the non-magical witches helped their families in their shops or found human work. Any brown witch could forage for herbs and prepare a tincture, but only one with magic could turn those tinctures into powerful healing elixirs. Just as any green witch could prepare a meal, but only the best could wield their magic to make the barest ingredients unforgettably delicious.

Heather took another sip of the warming tea, a spicy cinnamon flavor that lit up her tastebuds. A bright green wagon sat across the campfire with window boxes filled with herbs. They had converted the back gate into a raised garden bed filled to the brim with plants. Only a green witch could take any seed, plant it in any soil, and make a garden bloom.

"Here you are." Yasmin's voice snapped her back from gazing at the wagon. She held two chipped bowls in her hands.

"Thank you," Heather said, setting her mug by her feet to take the warm bowl from Yasmin's weathered hands. "I feel bad having you serve me."

The elderly witch shook her head. "I get the best deal in the carnival." She cackled and pat Heather smugly on the head. "There's nothing a green witch loves more than watching people enjoy her cooking. Plus, I get to make a huge mess and someone else has to clean it up." She gave Heather a wink and returned to the fire, where another green witch was holding out more bowls for her to serve.

"I like her," Heather murmured, taking a bite of stew.

Spices zinged across her tongue, creamy tomatoes and zesty black beans with a hint of citrus. The taste was so vibrant, she let out a low hum, closing her eyes to savor each flavor. When she opened her eyes again, she found Emry watching her, a faint flicker of red in her eyes. Heat crept up Heather's neck at that fiery gaze. Maybe she had been savoring her meal a little too loudly.

"I think I'm going to enjoy eating meals made by green

witches," Heather offered with a soft smirk, watching as a mirroring blush stained Emry's cheeks.

"I think I'm going to enjoy watching it," Emry rasped, lifting her thumb to wipe the corner of Heather's mouth.

Heather's fingers pressed tighter into the bowl to keep them from shaking. Laughter danced around them as the glow of the fire replaced the light of the setting sun. The warmth of the stew and hot drinks fended off the growing chill. As the moon rose, she thanked the Moon Goddess for sending her down this path. She'd get to do this every night —eat delicious dinners under star-filled skies with a beautiful red witch beside her.

CHAPTER FOUR

O nly a single candle flickered on the stovetop. Shadows loomed through the cluttered space as Heather turned in every direction. Sweat coated her palms as she clenched her hands together. Dinner had been amazing. The evening broke out into songs and story-telling around the fires. The moon rose high in the sky before they went to bed, and then Heather realized all at once: they were going to bed *together*.

She swallowed the lump in her throat as Emry climbed up the back ladder and onto the wooden floor, making the wagon shudder. The sight of her made Heather's heart drum a staccato beat. Emry had unbuttoned her shirt to the center of her chest, her sleeves rolled up and her suspenders stripped off her shoulders, hanging off her belt.

Heather bit the inside of her cheek, unable to stop herself from shifting from side to side. Emry was an utter and absolute goddess, and Heather was a nervous, clumsy fool.

Emry paused at a cabinet beside the stove. She opened it to reveal a tall, narrow wardrobe that rolled out into the room on a metal pole. Coats and shirts were crammed along the tiny line, so fused together they turned into one jumbled mess of linen and wool.

"I'll move some of my things out so you can hang up your clothes," Emry offered, pulling armfuls of garments out and chucking them on a box beside her. "I'll shuffle some things around. You'd be surprised how much space you can make with some ingenuity."

"I don't have that much," Heather insisted, staying Emry with a hand to her bicep. "I can unpack the rest in the morning."

Dark curls fell into Emry's eyes as she peered over her shoulder at Heather. "I usually change down here. Not much space up there." She tipped her head to the ladder that led to the lofted bed.

"Oh." Heather blushed, turning to give Emry privacy.

"That's not what I meant." Emry chuckled. "I just wanted you to know where everything was." She took a step toward Heather with a shrug. "This is your place now too. I want it to *feel* like yours."

Heather nodded, pressing her lips together as Emry took another step, then paused.

"Are you okay?" Emry asked with a cock of her head. "This is all too much for you, isn't it? We're all too much?" Emry worried her lip, and it was the first time Heather saw any concern on her face. "If-if this is all feeling like a lot and you're having regrets, it's okay to want to go home. There's a tavern at the next station where we could find pass—"

"No," Heather cut her off, the line of Emry's thoughts so counter to her own. "That's not what I want at all."

"Thank the Gods." Emry smirked, cupping her cheeks and pulling Heather's lips to her own.

The hair on her arms stood straight on end as Heather leaned her forehead against Emry's, breaking their kiss.

"It's been a long day. Are you tired?" Emry whispered, and Heather knew exactly what she was asking.

"I'm not tired." She took in a nervous breath. "But I . . . I've never done this before."

"We don't have to do anything, Heather." The sound of her name on Emry's lips made her stomach flip and heat creep through her body. "I'm so excited you're here, but I'm afraid I'm going to do or say something that'll scare you away. It's all so new and delicate and . . . Mother Moon, okay now I'm rambling."

Relief flooded through her as Emry scrambled to find her words. The slip of Emry's normal confident bravado made Heather smile. To know that Emry, too, was nervous made her feel a little more at ease.

"You won't scare me away," Heather said, threading her fingers through Emry's. A giddiness filled her at the sight of Emry's smile, knowing that she was the one to put it there. That happiness morphed to hunger as Emry's gaze dropped to Heather's lips, her mouth bridging the distance to land on hers again.

"What do you want?" Emry murmured against her mouth, and Heather knew if she said she wanted to sleep, Emry wouldn't care. But that wasn't what she wanted. Not as the yearning built white-hot in her core.

"I want to pick up where we left off the last time we were interrupted," Heather whispered, wrapping her hand around Emry's waist. A strange sort of pride raced through her that she had said it out loud. She felt older in that moment than she had in the breath before. She wanted Emry and she wouldn't let her nerves stop her.

～

Emry's firm hand bracketed her face, pulling her back into a kiss as her other hand snaked around her back. Their lips met in soft, slow kisses that sent tingles echoing through her body. Emry's tongue brushed across her lips and Heather opened for her, delighting in the low hum from Emry's chest as their tongues slid against each other.

The hand on her back slid down to her tailbone, urging Heather's hips tighter against Emry's own. That aching feeling grew as she pressed herself against Emry's muscled thigh, tilting her hips until the friction was setting her on fire.

"Yes," the word hissed out of Emry's lips as Heather moved against her.

Grinding wantonly, Heather moaned into Emry's mouth, and Emry replied with a corresponding sound and guided her backward onto the couch.

When Heather leaned back onto the cushions, Emry took a step back, hooded eyes watching Heather as she unbuttoned her own shirt. Lips parted, Heather watched, panting to catch her breath as Emry's shirt hung open, revealing the outline of her breasts and a strip of smooth tawny skin. Emry's cheeks dimpled as Heather stared indulgently at Emry's figure. She still couldn't believe this glorious witch wanted her—the little witch from the apothecary shop from a humdrum town in the west. But Heather forgot all of that when Emry's cat-like smile pulled at the edges and her eyes flickered crimson with lust-laced desire.

Heather reached for the hem of her dress and hauled the simple brown garment over her head, revealing her cotton slip beneath. Her nipples peaked through the gauzy fabric as Emry's gaze dropped, lingering over every inch as she took in her body.

"Mother Moon," Emry whispered like a prayer. "You are the most beautiful woman I've ever seen." She hurriedly whipped the rest of her shirt off and threw it to the floor, hastened by the sight of Heather pulling the thin straps of her slip over her shoulders. Emry met Heather's hands, taking over sliding the light fabric down her curving frame. Every cell in Heather's body homed into that touch as she lifted her hips and Emry trailed her slip down her thighs.

Heather lay back, forcing herself not to hide her naked form even as her cheeks burned traitorously. Emry made quick work of shucking her boots and removing her trousers, a mischievous grin spreading across her face as she prowled on top of Heather.

The feeling of Emry's warm skin against her own was electrifying. The feeling of Heather's curves pressed against Emry's muscled torso and soft breasts made her breath catch in her throat. Just the feeling of her skin was pushing her higher to an edge that she had only brought herself to before.

Fingers snaked around to the back of her neck and Emry's thumb stroked Heather's jaw. Emry gave her a featherlight kiss and pulled back to gaze at Heather with brilliant, glowing red eyes. Heather's hands flickered a faint bronze as she slid them up Emry's arms to her shoulders and, becoming more bold, down her back, tentatively stilling at the base of her spine. When Emry smiled wickedly, Heather's hands moved further, roving over her rounded backside. Emry's hooded, lust-filled eyes made Heather repeat the movement, trailing slow lines up and down her back, kneading the satin-soft skin all the way to the top of her thighs.

She paused as a flash of raw emotion passed over Emry's face. "What's wrong?"

"Nothing." Emry swept her thumb across Heather's cheek again. "I just . . . I've been through some things, terrible things, but saying goodbye to you was the worst moment of my life." Heather's fingers pressed tighter into Emry's warm flesh, pulling her flush against her body as if she could fuse the two of them together. "I know it is too soon to be saying such things—"

"It's not," Heather insisted, lifting her head to rest her forehead against Emry's. "I don't know what strange magic overcame me the moment I saw you, but it was stronger than any other magic I wield."

"Love is the strangest sort of magic." Emry laughed, dropping her head to Heather's ear. "And I know it's far too soon, but I need you to know, I love you, Heather."

"I need you to know I love you too," she whispered, body tingling at Emry's relieved breath.

It was the only word that could satisfy this maelstrom of feelings building inside her. Love. They loved each other, whether it was hasty or not. The instant her eyes landed on this beautiful carnival witch, something in her irrevocably changed, and she couldn't deny it any longer.

Emry slowly kissed her way down to Heather's neck, her tongue circling Heather's pulse and making her gasp. Emry let out a proud laugh as she rocked her hips into Heather. She trailed her mouth lower, down her collarbone and chest in teasing, slow kisses. Heather cupped the back of Emry's neck as she closed her mouth around her hardened nipple. With a moan, Heather arched into the sensation as Emry's tongue flicked over her.

Emry's hips rocked into her again and she responded, grinding into the hard muscle of her thigh between her legs. Warm desire spread through her from the top of her head to her toes. As Emry's tongue slowly circled her breast, her other reached up to work Heather's other nipple. It was a part of her body Heather had never thought to touch or explore, and yet she was panting, desperate for the sensations to continue.

The realization of what was happening pushed her even

higher. A pulsing need built between her legs, unlocking the last bits of restraint in her mind. She was in Emry's wagon. She'd really done it. Adventure stretched out before her with the most stunning and electrifying witch the world had ever seen . . . and she loved her. They loved each other.

That thought undid her. The surprise of her climax made her throw her head back, a low moan rumbling through her as she gripped tighter to Emry. With a final shudder, Emry released her mouth, trailing kisses back to the center of Heather's chest and down to her belly. Her light fingers stroked up and down Heather's thighs, sending bolts of desire straight to her core. She panted from her surprise release even as Emry lowered herself further.

"Do you want me to stop?" Emry murmured, lifting her lashes.

The need for more built in her instantly. Heat pooled at her core as she shook her head.

Emry pushed open her thighs with a smile. "Good. I'm not done exploring every inch of you yet."

Those glowing red eyes flicked up to Heather as her mouth hovered above her. Heather watched, breathless, as Emry lowered herself. Her breath brushed the hairs between Heather's legs and it took everything within her not to lift her hips and bridge the distance. Just the sight of Emry and the anticipation of what she was about to do made her ache so badly, another breathy groan escaped her lips.

The first stroke of Emry's tongue made her buck, and Emry let out a light chuckle.

"Steady," she said triumphantly as she pinned Heather's hips down with her forearm and worked her with her tongue. A deep groan echoed through Emry's chest, making her lips vibrate over Heather's tight bundle of nerves. Heather gripped the fabric of the couch so tightly she thought she might tear through it, clinging desperately as

Emry's tongue stroked her up and down. Her thighs shook and she couldn't stay still, the feeling so overwhelming she could hardly breathe. With her other hand, Emry touched the pad of her finger to Heather's hot, wet center. Slowly, she dipped her finger inside as her tongue kept moving.

Heather turned her face into the cushions as she cried out —a loud, mewling moan. Even muffled through the fabric, she wondered if the rest of the caravan might hear her shouts of ecstasy. Emry's finger massaged her, the rhythm of her hand matching the rhythm of her tongue until Heather forgot all the world existed except that lightning cloud of contact. As Emry added a second finger, stretching her in a way she never had been before, she bit into the pillow, uncaring if she shredded it with her teeth.

She bucked and squirmed and scrambled for purchase at the relentless building sensation in her. Just when she thought she reached the edge, it pushed even higher, spiraling into the stars of euphoria. The final groan from Emry's lips broke her. Her body clenched, her orgasm slamming through her as she screamed into the pillow. On and on, it tore through her, so much bigger and brighter than the first. That release flashed through every corner of her body, pulling cries of ecstasy from her until her voice went hoarse.

Heather's muscles finally went slack, and she collapsed back down into the cushions. She was boneless and elated all at once. Emry prowled back up her body, a look of endless pride on her face. Her eyes flared such a brilliant shade of scarlet that it lit the entire cabin.

Burying her head in Heather's neck, Emry whispered, "I love you."

"I love you too," she said again, relishing in saying those words. Heather smiled, chest still heaving as she pulled Emry close. "Mother Moon, that was . . ."

"Just the beginning," Emry murmured into her neck.

Heather's heart skipped a beat as the echoes of her orgasm still rolled through her. She traced a hand down Emry's spine and whispered, "I want you to show me everything."

Emry's teeth nibbled on Heather's ear. "Happy to oblige."

CHAPTER FIVE

Five days later

≈

She wrapped her shawl around her shoulders, watching the whorls of steam curl into the midnight air. Heather sat at the back of the wagon, her feet dangling as the strange grasses swished around her feet. Nothing was like home. The trees were shaped differently. The birdsong had a sharp, whining twitter, and it smelled of red clay and sunbaked earth. The excitement of the day slowed as the stars twinkled above her, stretching endlessly into the night. It was the most open expanse she'd ever seen. The fairgrounds in Valtene were big, but this . . . the savanna spilled over the horizon out to the thin strip of moon-kissed ocean in the far distance.

She'd never seen the ocean before. Its vastness was unfathomable—the way it drifted off so far until it blurred into the skyline. Her siblings would never believe her if she tried to describe it.

A quiet ache grew in her chest, as if her body could feel the distance between her and the rest of the Doledir family. She wondered if her mother was brushing her sisters' hair now and if their prayers to Mother Moon felt different without Heather. Did they miss her as much as she missed them?

She combed her fingers through her loose hair, dividing it into three solid strands. She braided her copper-red locks, imagining it was her mother's hands. As she whispered a prayer to the night sky, she pictured her mother whispering the same words to the same bright moon. A tear slipped from the corner of her eye and trailed down her cheek.

The shuffling of bare feet announced Emry's arrival. She silently sat beside Heather, watching the stars. Finishing her braid, Heather tied it as another tear slipped down her cheek. She sniffed, trying to stymy the tears, but the sound made Emry move. Wrapping her arms around Heather, she pulled her into a tight hug.

The feeling of her arms around her made the tears fall heavier. She buried her head into Emry's shoulder, that strange feeling of loss coursing through her. Emry rubbed slow, soothing circles down her back as Heather cried. It was a sharp, sudden burst of emotions, the surge retreating as quickly as it came forth.

"I'm okay." Heather wiped her eyes as she pulled away. "I just miss them."

"I know." Emry wiped a rogue tear off Heather's lips with her thumb. "I miss my family sometimes too, despite the fact they are not nearly as lovely as your own."

Heather gave a half-hearted smile. She knew what a blessing it was to have her family. The Doledirs were a tight-knit bunch—a chaotic house filled with love. She hoped her departure wouldn't change that—that, even with distance, she would always feel close to them.

She prayed again they would forgive her for leaving when her father was so ill. Pa would take the blame, she was certain of it. A small smile played on her lips as she imagined him telling them how he shoved her out the door, shouting at her and demanding that she go. He would tell them that he wanted her to go sell their wares in Saxbridge, that good coin was to be made and that it was a business decision and therefore *his* to make. Heather had no say in it.

Rose would probably see through his over-exuberant lies, but the others would believe him. Heather loved her father for that. He was already protecting the relationships of his children for when he was no longer around.

"I don't want to go back," Heather murmured, clearing her throat. "I just wish they didn't feel so far."

"I know." Emry rubbed the tail of Heather's copper braid between her fingers. "You can feel excited and sad about your choices all at once. The best decisions are never easy ones."

Heather leaned over and brushed a soft kiss to Emry's lips. The soft press of her mouth was already so familiar after only a handful of days. The rhythms of carnival life were becoming familiar too, and Heather was surprised how quickly she'd settled into the eccentric carnival lifestyle.

Emry cupped Heather's cheek and whispered, "Wait here."

She disappeared down the long alley of crates into the heart of the wagon. When she returned, she held a book and a quill in a pottle of ink. Careful not to spill the ink, she sat back beside Heather and ripped a sheet of blank paper from her book.

"We'll be passing through Castleview tomorrow. They have a traveling postmaster there." Emry set the paper atop the book and handed it to Heather.

Swallowing the lump in her throat, Heather's eyes welled again. She nodded, afraid if she spoke, the tears would start falling again.

As if sensing her thoughts, Emry said, "There's plenty more blank pages in that book if you smudge this one."

Tapping the quill on the ink well, Heather already knew she'd need another sheet of paper. It had been only a few days, and she already had so much to tell them—so much of the world she'd seen, so many new animals, and foods, and stories, and customs. If this was all happening within her own court, what would the rest of Okrith hold?

She opened the blanket around her shoulders and wrapped the other half around Emry. Scooting closer, Emry folded the other side around them. They huddled together, sharing warmth, as Emry star-gazed and Heather readied the quill. Emry's silent presence soothed the unease in Heather's soul, a new steadiness finding her again anchored to the person beside her. Even in her sadness, she felt overwhelmed with joy. She'd felt more bigger and deeper emotions in the past five days than the rest of her life combined. There was a sense of rightness in her soul—this was the start of a new beginning that she would look back upon fondly for the rest of her life.

She lowered ink to paper and wrote, *"Dear Family . . ."*

CHAPTER SIX

Two Weeks Later

The *Carnivale du Fareas* stopped in the coastal town of Southport. Built at the bottom of the cliff, Southport's switchback trails led up to the red hills where the witches parked their spiral of wagons. The allure of the vistas had pulled Heather to the edge of the red rocks to stare out at the ocean below. The Sea of Callipho was a glittering cerulean world unto itself. The southernmost tip of the Western Court was filled with slender trees, sunbaked red earth and plants with needle-like spikes. Briny air swirled around her, granting a reprieve from the heat.

Emry's arms snaked around her torso, and Heather realized she was still staring at the miniature white sails on the horizon.

"Sorry," Heather whispered, a smile pulling on her lips. "I got distracted."

"It's your first time seeing the ocean." Emry kissed her temple. "I can finish setting up the stall."

"No, I should be helping. It's my first time running the stall too." Heather's braid whipped behind her as she turned back toward the fairgrounds. "I want to show you I can do it. Besides, I have a feeling I'll be seeing the ocean again now that I'm with you."

That made Emry's smile broaden, but still she said, "Enjoy the views." She put her hand to Heather's hip, stalling her. "You can help the next time. They'll be plenty more opportunities."

Emry's short hair had coiled into tighter curls in the humidity, her smooth skin deepening a shade. Her tunic unbuttoned to the center of her chest, the burgundy fabric stained with sweat. Heather's eyes hooked on a bead that trailed between Emry's breasts and she fought the urge to slide her fingers down the same path.

Emry's eyes flickered a crimson red as her cheeks dimpled. "Whatever you're thinking," she rasped, her voice dropping an octave, "hang onto it. I have somewhere I want to show you tonight."

"You ready for your first day?" Drea called from her wagon, holding the brim of her tricorne hat against the wind. The *Carnivale du Fareas's* leader had grown up in Southport. It made sense now why she dressed more like a seafaring trader than a carnival witch.

"I think so," Heather called back and then immediately chewed her bottom lip, belying any confidence in her words. She had no idea what the day would entail. There seemed to be an art to selling to passersby that she didn't understand. In the apothecary, everyone came to her. She didn't need to hang her head out the window and beckon people in. She didn't need to convince them to buy anything. No, this was different.

Emry's arm dropped around Heather's shoulder, pulling her from the chaos of her thoughts. "She's ready," Emry said confidently.

Drea's eyes narrowed, snagging on something on the horizon. She hopped down from her wagon and ambled down the dusty trail to where they stood. Gravel crunched beneath her boots as she stared out from the cliffside and down toward her hometown and the sea beyond.

"That one," she said, pointing to a ship so far out that Heather had to squint to see it. "That one could be trouble for us."

"It doesn't look any different from the others," Heather questioned.

Drea huffed, looking at Heather like she had two heads.

"Shadow Blades?" Emry asked, and Drea nodded. "Shit."

"Are they pirates?" Heather gasped, watching the ship sailing into port.

"Of sorts." Drea scowled. "Seafaring bandits. They're thieves, but mostly harmless unless you corner one of them. Much like the snakes in these parts," she added with a wink

Heather gulped. "Mostly harmless?"

"Let's pray they're turning east toward Silver Sands," Drea said, clutching her totem pouch around her neck and looking up toward the sky.

Emry leaned further into Heather, her fingers pressing into Heather's arm in reassurance. "I can handle a few Shadow Blades."

"Oh, believe me, I know." Drea flashed a grin between the two of them and then patted Heather on the shoulder. "Make us proud today."

Heather bobbed her chin, tucking a stray strand of her copper hair behind her ear. When Drea disappeared behind her wagon, she leaned into Emry. The letters in her pocket crinkled at the movement.

"What did they say?" Emry asked, her gaze dropping to Heather's pocket.

Her parents had sent a letter ahead to Southport after Heather told them in her latest correspondence where the carnival would be stopping for the week.

When the messenger arrived that morning with an armful of letters, she had hoped one would be for her. Still, when they called her name, she couldn't help the tears that fell. Holding the worn edges of that letter was like holding a piece of her family, and all the homesickness she thought she had overcome over the last few weeks came flooding back.

"They're doing well," Heather said, voice thickening. "Preparing for the winter months. They had their first snow." She breathed in the sea air, the scorching sun heating her skin. "I can't believe that it's snowing in the same Court at this very moment."

"The many climates of the Western Court—heavy snow and drizzly rain all the way to scorched deserts and savanna." Emry's eyes roved the dusty red horizon and back down toward the wharf. "How's your father?"

"All he said was he was doing well and enjoying that the shop was slowing down for the winter," Heather said.

She knew it was a deliberate omission to make no mention of his ailing health. But the further they ventured from her hometown of Valtene, the more she knew the truth: if his health declined, she wouldn't be able to make it back in time, whether he wanted her to or not. Knowing it wasn't even an option made her ache. They'd already said their goodbyes for however long in the future, but it still hurt to think about.

Emry pulled Heather tighter into her body and kissed the top of her head. "And your siblings?"

She breathed in Emry's scent, tinted with a hint of the

lavender salve she'd fashioned for her. "Oliver, Evelyn, and Cole all added their own little notes."

"And Rose?"

Heather could only imagine her sister's shocked and bitter face when she found out Heather had left. Even so, she didn't think Rose would be so angry about it. Only a year her junior, her little sister had always wanted to run the Doledir Apothecary. She had more business sense and a disciplined work ethic. She'd keep the shop running well after their father passed.

She hung her head, toeing the gravel beneath her boots. "Rose was entirely absent from their updates."

"Why does that not surprise me?" Emry chuckled, shaking her head and giving Heather a comforting squeeze. "Give her time. She'll come around, eventually."

"And if she doesn't?" Heather took a step out of Emry's touch, heading back up toward their wagon.

Emry didn't miss a step, falling into stride with her. "Then it's her loss."

There was no comfort in that sentiment through and anxiety bloomed in Heather's gut. What if Rose wasn't content with ruining their own relationship? What if, once their father was gone, Rose drove a wedge between the rest of the family and Heather? She tried to focus on the day at hand, but she knew she'd be stewing on that ominous thought regardless.

CHAPTER SEVEN

By midday, the heat was unbearable. Heather clung to the shade of the wagon, fanning herself with a box lid in between mixing tinctures. Ravi perched above her, surveying the crowd as Emry chatted with patrons. They fell into an easy routine, Emry taking the sales position at the front of the stall while Heather mixed orders and restocked from the back. Emry easily beckoned people to their table with her cavalier confidence, then Heather listened to their maladies and produced the right vial to treat them. Within hours, their coin box was overflowing and half the bottles on the table had disappeared. It seemed many a person in Southport was in need of a skilled witch healer; several vowed to return the following day with family members and friends. Heather raced about refilling the baskets of herbs until the blistering sun demanded she slow down.

The people of Southport wore light linen fabrics, carrying parasols of woven flax to shade themselves from the sweltering heat. Heather had hoped the crowds would thin when the sun was highest in the sky, retreating to the shade, but with a witch carnival in town, they all braved the weather to shop the stalls.

She had thought it would be hard to sell her simple remedies, but no matter where people came from, they all had similar afflictions: trouble sleeping, rashes, upset stomach, toothaches . . . They were the tonics and salves that kept an apothecary in business, and the people of Southport were eager for the services of "the best brown witch in the Western Court" as Emry loudly proclaimed.

Taking advantage of the brief pause in the crowds, Emry lifted the heavy coin box up and looked over her shoulder at Heather. "I'm going to take this to Drea. Empty it out before the afternoon rush."

"Afternoon rush?" This wasn't already the afternoon rush? Heather peeked up, fanning herself to see Emry tuck the coin box under her arm. Judging by the strain of her muscles, it was heaving with silver *druni*.

"There's always last-minute stragglers who want to buy something before we close for the day. Make sure to drink some water," Emry reminded with a wink.

Heather nodded, watching as the red witch disappeared through the thick crowds. She ambled over to the lone stool and perched, taking the head place at their table. Luckily, most of the throng were busy shopping other stalls—embroidered totem pouches, glass baubles, and petting the giant yellow snake wrapped around Ean Mallor's shoulders.

She spotted Yasmin pushing through the crowd, holding aloft a tray of spun sugar treats. She wore a thick belt with pouches of jangling coins and braided flax dolls to hand out to the children. Parents stopped her every few paces to buy sweets for their eager witchlings. Despite her stooped, aging frame, her arm muscles were surprisingly strong, working the crowds with ease.

The way the carnival witches delighted was a magic all its

own. A buzzing fell over the *Carnivale du Fareas* when they opened up shop. The witches' smiles were wider, excitement charging the air. Heather wondered what it would be like when they finally ventured to Saxbridge for the winter. They'd stop there for three whole moon cycles, selling to both witches and the rich fae who holidayed in the warmer climate. It was the longest stint the carnival spent anywhere. The rest of the year they traveled, circling Okrith only to end up in Saxbridge for the following winter. It probably felt like a lifetime to stay in one place for a traveling witch.

Ravi cawed, pulling Heather from her musings, as a shadow covered the front row of vials. Heather squinted up to see a strange-looking human man. Eyes lined with kohl and weathered pale skin, he wore fisherman's garb of a stained white shirt and threadbare black trousers. But the thin golden chains that hung around his neck and circled his fingers gave her pause—so at odds with the rattiness of his attire. A head taller than the rest of the crowd, he had high cheekbones and a sharp jawline, with a broad, muscular physique—too wide for the lean build of the seafaring types. A chill zipped down her spine. This wasn't a regular fisherman.

He gave Heather a crooked smile. "Hello."

"How can I help you?" she asked, her eyes dropping to the obsidian dagger on his belt. The sunlight glinted off its serrated steel teeth.

Her stomach lurched. Was this one of the Shadow Blades that Drea spoke of? Whoever he was, he didn't seem like any witch she'd ever met before, let alone a normal shopper.

She peered down to the stalls on either side of her, the rest of the witches still selling to patrons, their attentions lost in the crowds of people.

"I'm looking for something," he murmured, his gnarled fingers mindlessly picking through the baskets of herbs.

"Do you know what it's called?" Heather tried to keep her voice polite and steady even as she clenched her hands tighter behind her back. Her mind whirled with ways to defend herself but always came up lacking. A little pocket knife lay in a crate below the table, used to cut twine and unwrap parcels . . . but against that dagger? Why had the other witches not spotted this mountain of a man? Perhaps he just seemed ominous?

The man lifted his smudged onyx eyes to her. "Some call it witches' gold."

Her eyes widened. *Bonebane*. It was a toxic waxy-leafed plant with golden flowers found in only remote mountain regions of the Western Court. Heather's very own great-great-grandmother had been the first one to discover its medicinal properties, though some now abused the substance. She could tell by the man's dilated eyes that he had probably already imbibed something. It was certainly an expensive poison to procure.

Meant to aid the dying, it was only given to patients with mere days—maybe a week—left because it was so highly addictive. How to prepare the bonebane was also a tightly kept brown witch secret for fear of people using it to murder others. When mixed with certain other flowers such as blooming amethyst, the poison could be inhaled or absorbed through the skin. Rose and Heather had to swear an oath to the moon to even learn about all of its properties from their father.

"I'm sorry, we don't carry any of that." Heather did a terrible job of not reacting to the mention of bonebane as she shook her head and feigned a pleasant voice. "How about redbank cyclamen? What ailment are you in need of remedying?"

The man slammed his fist down on the table, making the glasses clink together and Heather jolt backward. Ravi cawed louder at the sound, but above the clamor of the throng, Emry probably wouldn't be able to hear him.

"No matter, little dove." The man's smile didn't meet his eyes, his carefree words not matching his erratic movements. He glanced over his shoulder to another impossibly tall man pushing through the crowd.

Heather's heart leapt into her throat. His comrade wore the same kohl lining his eyes and black dagger on his hip. Her eyes darted wildly through the press of fairgoers and spotted three more disappearing into the crowd like water disappearing into desert sand.

The man tracked her line of sight and snickered, drawing her gaze back to him. He picked up a vial off the table, waggled it in front of her, and put it in his pocket without breaking their stare.

Heather sucked in a breath, not knowing what to say. But her internal debate was short-lived as someone screamed, "Fire!"

Her head whipped toward the farthest wagon in the spiral, Benton's wagon. A thin trail of inky smoke swirled into the sky. With nothing but scrub brush and wooden carriages around them, the whole place would be ablaze in minutes if they didn't act quickly. She took a step toward the fire when the man's hand shot out, his jagged blade held out at eye level.

He flashed a smile of yellow rancid teeth as he bent until his foul mouth reached her ear. His voice dropped into a low whisper. "I'll give you three seconds to run."

CHAPTER EIGHT

Heather's stomach roiled as she stared at the black dagger pointed menacingly at her throat.

"One," the Shadow Blade counted as her hands trembled.

The witches all around her abandoned their stalls and ran to help put out the fire, the crowd quickly thinning into nothingness.

Shit. The thieves were drawing them away from their wagons to make them easier to loot.

"Two." The man took a step to the side of the table, keeping his blade aloft.

Ravi screeched and dove down, attacking the man, who flailed trying to shoo the bird away. Who needed a guard dog when you had a feisty raven? Heather didn't wait for her attacker to inch closer, and she certainly didn't wait for him to count to *three*. She thanked the Goddess for that raven and made a mental note to build him an even bigger perch as she turned and bolted.

Heather turned the corner and pushed through a group of confused stragglers and screamed, "Run!"

Chaos erupted all around her as people ran from the fire and ran from her screams. None of them knew if they were racing from danger or straight into it. Waves of fleeing witches scattered in every direction. One collided headlong into Heather, bowling her over. Her feet flew skyward from the force of the collision and her shoulder crashed into the unyielding red earth. Instinctively, her arms shielded her head, worried she'd be trampled. She could hear Drea barking orders to some of the carnival witches, the screeching roar of the fire rising above people's screams.

A shadow loomed over her again, and she peered up at the smirking face of the man from the stall. Her gaze narrowed at him and she gasped as he morphed before her very eyes. His frame widened even more and his features turned sharper. Gone were his rounded human ears, and in their place, slender pointed ones appeared.

Heather's stomach plummeted as she took him in.

He was fae.

Chest heaving, Heather gaped at the fae hovering above her. She'd never been this close to one of their kind before . . . unless they'd been glamoured like he had been moments before. That thought made bile rise up her throat. Maybe she had met a fae before without even knowing?

Something about him had felt so off, but she had chalked it up to him being a ruffian.

The Shadow Blade admired his dagger with appreciation before casting his gaze down to Heather, still panting in the dust. "Didn't get far, did you, love?"

As he took a step forward, Heather grabbed a handful of gravel and flung it at his face. He retreated a step with a growl, then inched closer as he wiped the grit from his eyes. Heather seized the opportunity and fortuitous angle by kicking him hard in the groin. He doubled over just as Heather rose into a crouch and shot upward. She threw out a clumsy punch, but it collided with his mouth. She scrambled back to her feet, thanking the Moon Goddess for having four younger siblings who always were trying to scrap with her as kids and didn't care about fighting dirty. She wouldn't win a fight with a fae, but at least it would buy her enough time to flee.

She raced toward the center of the spiral where Drea's wagon sat. The twisting paths between the wagons were now vacant, the patrons all having fled downhill back to South-port and away from the blaze. People living in such arid conditions probably knew the dangers a fire presented all too well. Little did they know, the Shadow Blades were hiding amongst the chaos.

The crunching footsteps of the Shadow Blade chased Heather as she wove through the wagons, bolting like a spooked doe. He'd lost his line of sight on her as the spiral tightened toward the center, but he was faster and this path led to a dead end. Making a decision without slowing, she ducked behind a bright yellow wagon and dropped, crawling on her belly underneath. She tried to quiet her panting breaths, each desperate gasp kicking up dust around her sweaty face.

The center of the spiral was silent. Not a single pair of boots appeared from under the wagon's floor. She guessed that the rest of *Carnivale du Fareas* was at the edge of the spiral, helping put out the fire. They probably confused the pandemonium as people fleeing the fire. Did they even know who hid amongst them? Meanwhile, those Shadow Blades ransacked their wagons. She needed to warn them.

Pulling herself to the edge of the wagon, she waited again, her ears ringing in the quiet. Faint shouts in the distance called for buckets of water. She took one more steadying breath, preparing to run. But before she could move, a hand wrapped around her ankle.

CHAPTER NINE

Heather shrieked as the hand holding her ankle yanked her backward. She clawed against that tugging to no avail, her fingernails scraping across the dry earth, but she was easily yanked out from underneath the wagon. Before she could blink back the dust, she was roughly lifted by the collar of her dress. Her back slammed against the side of the wagon, and a wicked, grinning face leaned close to hers.

"Think you can hide from me, little dove?" the Shadow Blade asked, cocking his head. A thin rivulet of blood trailed from his split lip down to his chin. She'd done that. His wide crazed eyes roved her fearful face.

Tears welled as terror gripped her, eyes snagging on that ominous blade.

"Shh." The fae's grin pulled at his wounded lip, but he didn't flinch. Already it was healing, the bleeding stopping right before her eyes. It was the first time she'd ever seen the incredible magic of fae healing close-up. "I'm a bandit, not a murderer." He lifted his eyebrows at her in stern warning.

"Now, don't dart off again, and you'll make it out of this in one piece, alright?"

Before she could nod, he whirled her around, pinning her back to his chest with his dagger at her throat. A tear slipped down Heather's cheek as he jostled her into the center of the spiral through the upturned benches and cold fire pit.

Drea appeared, rushing with an empty bucket toward her wagon. When she spotted them, she skidded to a halt, water sloshing over the bucket's rim.

"There you are, Yirloana." The fae's chest vibrated against Heather's back, his foul breath clinging to her hair.

"Veltis," Drea shouted, balling her fists. "I should've known that fire was your doing."

"You're getting slow in your old age, *witch*," Veltis boomed. "Now go fetch that chest in your wagon."

Drea folded her arms and popped out her hip, surprisingly cavalier considering Heather had a knife to her throat.

"What chest?" Drea asked.

"Don't play with me." Veltis jostled Heather, making her yelp. "I know you keep the carnival's coffers in there. We both know I'm not leaving here without it."

Another figure came racing between the wagons as Heather's pulse thundered in her ears. She knew who it was before her shadow even emerged through the wagons. For a second, she wondered if she'd suddenly gained the blue witches' intuition, the clarity with which she knew who it was. As if a rope connected one to the other, she felt the tightening of the slack and knew she was coming for her.

Emry.

The red witch's eyes and hands flamed more vividly than Heather had ever seen. A frightening expression morphed her face from fear to one of pure wrath as she stared from Veltis to the knife in his hand.

"Let. Her. Go." Emry seethed, fiery fingers curling into fists. "Now."

Heather shuddered at the venom in her words. Emry was suddenly the embodiment of the mighty and fearsome red witches.

"Is she yours, then?" Veltis guffawed. He tipped his head to Drea but kept his eyes on Emry. "I'll let your lover go when your captain gets my coins. Don't dillydally, let's go."

He gestured with his dagger for Drea to get a move on.

Mistake.

The second his dagger left the sensitive flesh of Heather's throat, it flew from his hands as if on an invisible string. Emry's red witch magic turned into an inferno. The black dagger hovered, circling back toward the fae and angling toward his left eye.

Veltis hastily released his grip on Heather, and she bolted forward, racing to Emry's side.

"Call your Blades off or lose an eye, Veltis," Drea called with a victorious grin.

He let out a high whistle, and five Shadow Blades emerged from the wagons, darting uphill toward the ridge at his signal.

Veltis kept his attention fixed on the dagger hovering an inch from his eye.

"I should take this just so you remember never to threaten a witch," Emry snarled, the dagger inching forward until it was a hair's breadth away.

Veltis's broad body trembled like a sapling in a strong wind. He dared not move, not breathe, as he waited for Emry's judgment. The dagger pulled away and clattered to the ground.

Veltis's whole body sagged in relief.

"Consider this your lucky day, Veltis," Drea shouted. "Now go before we change our minds."

He fled before she even finished speaking, scurrying away like a dog with his tail between his legs.

As he disappeared through the wagons, Emry grabbed Heather and pulled her into a crushing hug. The air was squeezed from Heather's lungs, but she didn't care as she squeezed Emry back just as tightly.

"Are you okay?" Her voice was muffled in Heather's hair.

Heather nodded, panicked tears slipping down her cheeks as she tried to slow her thundering pulse.

"I'm okay," she whispered, even as her body purged the adrenaline coursing through her veins. "Benton's wagon?"

"A few boards will need replacing, but we caught the fire before it got out of control. All are accounted for. Uninjured apart from nearly you." Emry buried her head into the crook of Heather's neck and murmured against her skin, "I'm so sorry. I should've been there."

"You can't always be right next to me." Heather swept a soothing hand down her back, comforting her just as much.

"I can try."

Heather chuckled, pulling away from Emry just enough to rest their foreheads together. "Teach me how to fight."

Emry's eyebrows shot up. "What?"

"I need to protect myself," Heather said, stooping and picking up the Shadow Blade's discarded dagger. "Teach me."

"All right." Emry smirked, carefully taking the weapon from her grasp. "But we're not going to start with something so . . . lethal. We can keep this in the wagon for one day when you're ready."

Heather nodded, worrying her lip.

"Looks like you got a good hit on him before I even arrived." Emry placed her finger under Heather's chin, lifting her face until she met Emry's storming crimson gaze. "I'm proud of you."

Heather lifted on her toes and brushed a kiss to Emry's

lips. That sweet contact made the horrors of the attack fade into the background. Everything felt safe when Emry's lips were on hers. Everything felt quiet and calm and beautiful.

With a long sigh, Emry broke their kiss. "Well, come on, then."

Heather quirked her brow, watching as Emry began walking back toward their wagon. "What?"

"Seeing as they scared all the patrons off, we might as well start training now."

Drea chuckled from where she leaned against her wagon. Shaking her head, she gave Heather a wink. "Go easy on her, Heather."

CHAPTER TEN

The leaves rustled on a soft wind as they walked from stone to stone down the winding red path. They followed the narrowing trail as it pierced into the cliff's face. The jutting rocks formed a makeshift path that ran through the water-bogged gravel. Sun scalded the rock from high above, but the crevice shaded them from its relentless rays.

"Where are we going?" Heather's voice echoed up the jagged stone.

"To train."

"Are we sure we won't encounter any more trouble out here?"

They'd been walking for nearly half an hour down toward the sea. The sounds of the carnival and Southport faded far out of earshot until all they could hear were the faint rolling waves and caw of gulls.

"The Shadow Blades are long gone," Emry said, balancing her hand against the rock wall as she stepped from stone to stone. "They probably are halfway up the Western coast by now."

"They're awful."

"Bandits usually are." Emry huffed. "They used to keep to the seaside towns but are getting bolder, moving inland."

"I've never met a fae up close before," Heather murmured.

"Not a pleasant lot, are they?"

"They can't all be that bad." Heather kept her eyes on her feet, careful not to slip into the shallow water around the path. She wondered if the whole path was dry at low tide. "That one, Veltis, said they were looters, not murderers."

"I'm sure he feels comforted by that distinction," Emry snarled, and Heather was certain by her flare of magic that she was reliving the attack. "It's not the Shadow Blades I fear most, but the first fae royal who realizes they can turn them into a weapon."

"What?"

The path forked, and, as they twisted down toward the right, the water grew deeper.

"A disorganized crew with *flexible* morals is ripe for a fae patron to come and bankroll their escapades for their own gains." Emry clicked her tongue as she shucked her boots and slung them over her shoulder by their laces.

Heather followed Emry's lead and took her boots off too. "Who would do such a thing?"

"How much do you know of the fae?"

"Not much," Heather replied honestly.

She knew of the five courts and the five ruling families: Thorne, Emberspear, Norwood, Vostemur, and Dammacus. She knew the fae were physically stronger and faster than the witches, and had finely tuned senses and rapid healing. She also knew that lucky witches were hired by rich fae patrons. It had been her father's hope that some of her siblings might find patronage with a rich fae family as their personal brown witch healer, but Heather had only encountered a few in person only in passing or at a distance . . . apart from Veltis.

Emry let out a soft grumble. "With a steady stream of fae gold in their pockets, I think the Shadow Blades will forget the distinction between looters and murderers real quick."

Heather furrowed her brow, considering those words as her fingers idly trailed across the red stone. "You think Queen Thorne will hire them as assassins?"

"She should get a handle on them if she was smart," Emry said. "Before the Vostemurs or Norwoods get their claws in them. A roving band of fae scoundrels? Mother Moon, one might start a war with them at their beck and call."

Heather had to leap to reach the next step without slipping, which was submerged in ankle-deep water. Arms flailing to the side, she nearly fell before Emry grabbed her by the arm and steadied her.

Emry chuckled, her voice echoing off the stone. "We're not swimming . . . yet."

"I thought you were going to train me to fight?"

"I am."

The darkness swallowed them as they entered the narrow cave mouth. Heather's eyes strained to adjust to the sudden darkness. Her hands skimmed over the damp rock, feeling her way. Their heavy breaths and sloshing feet ricocheted off the low ceiling, and the sound of lapping water grew as they emptied out into a vast opening.

Heather's feet halted when they reached dry rock again, and she sucked in a breath. Starlight twinkled high above them . . . no, not starlight. The constellations of silvery blue were coming from the craggy roof of the cave.

"What . . ." Her mouth hung open as she stared at the beautiful, eerie glow.

"Have you never seen glowworms before?"

Heather's eyebrows shot up. "I've seen fireflies before . . . but nothing like this."

"Come on," Emry said, hauling her tunic over her head. "Let's train."

The sight of the smooth lines of Emry's stomach that flared to a soft curve in her hips finally snapped Heather's focus. Her eyes traced over Emry's dark undervest and down to where her fingers unbuckled her belt. Heather bit her lip as Emry hooked her thumbs in her unbuttoned trousers and pushed them down, revealing her fitted black undershorts.

"Training first." Emry cleared her throat, her voice having grown husky with desire.

With the promise of pleasure hanging in the air between them, Heather knew training would be the sweetest torture.

CHAPTER ELEVEN

"Take off anything you don't want to get wet."

"Too late," Heather said, frowning at the damp hem of her skirt.

Pressing her lips together, Heather unbuttoned her dress down to her chest and slipped it off her shoulders. The fabric pooled around her feet, and she stepped out into her thin white slip that skimmed her mid-thigh.

Emry stooped, gathering her clothes and Heather's dress. She paused to brush a kiss to the inside of Heather's knee before standing. Lightning coursed through Heather at that featherlight touch.

Emry hung their clothes on a rocky outcrop and leapt to a stone in the middle of the dark pool. The glowing light illuminated the still water with a silvery hue. Emry stepped to the next rock along and turned back to Heather, beckoning her with a hand.

Heather jumped to the first of the two rocks, bare feet landing on the cool stone. They stood on their little pedestals, facing each other in a sea of briny obsidian water.

Without warning, Emry's arm swung out, pushing

Heather to the side. Squealing, Heather windmilled her arms, but she couldn't keep herself upright and went toppling into the pool. The cool ocean water was a shock to her warm skin. She brushed the stray hairs that escaped her braid off her face, arms swirling around her as she frowned up at Emry.

The silvery glow lit up Emry's eyes as she smirked down at Heather. "First lesson: balance."

Heather gave her a mock scowl and hoisted herself back up onto the slippery rock. Her thin slip clung to her body, her nipples peaking through the sheer fabric. Emry surveyed her with a wolflike grin.

"Training first," Heather echoed her own words, and Emry cleared her throat again.

"Right." She sighed, stretching as if she could ease the ache Heather knew was building in her core. "Look at my feet. See how I'm standing?"

Heather mirrored Emry's position.

"Good." Emry nodded. "And bend your knees a little more, sink down. You want to feel grounded in place. Yes, like that."

She repeated the sweeping movement, tapping Heather's shoulder, but this time Heather could hold her ground.

"Feel the difference?"

Heather nodded.

"I want you to block my strikes without breaking this stance, okay?" Emry asked, her hands moving slowly as she swung a mock punch toward Heather.

Heather lifted her hand to block, keeping her feet firmly planted. Then another and another. Emry's arms swept through the air as if moving through water. Heather lost herself in the rhythm of it, when Emry suddenly struck out again and Heather toppled back into the cold water.

When her head breached the surface, Emry said, "Keep your knees bent."

Heather grumbled a curse under her breath and pulled herself back up onto her rock. Water dripped down her limbs, her slip clinging to her curves.

A low growl escaped Emry's lips as she surveyed Heather's body again. Heather knew she wasn't the stronger fighter, but a wry smile pulled on her lips at that lustful look in Emry's eyes. In many ways, she still had the upper hand. Heather smoothed the fabric down her figure, lifting the hem to wring out the water, knowing it would make the slip cling to her body like a second skin.

"Train later," Emry groaned, and tackled Heather back into the pool.

The rush of water colliding with her back cut off Heather's laugh. The second they broke the surface, Emry's lips were on hers, pinning her backward against the edge of the rock pool.

Heather broke their kiss with a laugh. "You're not a very disciplined teacher, you know."

"Can you blame me?" Emry's lips found her neck, and she sucked and nibbled her way up to Heather's ear. Each movement sent aching pulses straight to her core. "Ean can teach you to fight. I'm going to be too distracted."

Emry's wanton lips silenced Heather's laugh. She scooted Heather's hips up onto the submerged ledge leading out of the rock pool. Sliding up the hem of Heather's wet slip, Emry yanked it over her head and chucked it into a corner of the cave. A low hum of pleasure rumbled through Emry's chest as she prowled up the algae-covered rock, inching Heather backward until she lay to the side of her.

The tide pool swirled around Heather's hair, breasts, belly, and hips, breaking above the surface as the velvety smooth rock held them aloft. Emry's hand snaked down

Heather's body as her lips found hers again. She trailed over her breasts in slow, taunting circles, her hand drifting lower as Heather lifted her hips, trying to draw those fingers to right where she needed them to be.

Every moment with Emry had been a frenzy. A constant aching need for her filled her days and was sated only through their long nights in their wagon. She knew one day that constant yearning would ebb into a slower, steadier kind of love, but right then she wanted Emry endlessly. The burning look in her glowing eyes matched the flames igniting her desire.

Bending one knee, Heather lifted her hips higher out of the water, desperate for Emry's touch. A deep moan escaped her lips at the first stroke of Emry's fingers. They slid in slow, teasing movements, up and down. Tingles of pleasure zipped from Heather's throbbing bud straight down to her toes.

Emry's mouth swallowed Heather's moans as Heather's hips ground into her hand, urging Emry to move faster. She didn't want to go slow. Her hand dipped into the waistband of Emry's undershorts, and Emry's rhythm stumbled as Heather's fingers parted her flesh and slid down her slick center.

They groaned in unison, fingers circling each other in the ways they knew the other liked. Emry's fingers moved lower, dipping inside of Heather and making her suck in a sharp breath, the sensation of being filled overtaking her. They pushed each other higher with the sound of their joined rapture. Heather moved her fingers faster, circling Emry's sweet bundle of nerves as Emry's fingers pumped her core.

Her moans grew more desperate, her muscles straining as she pushed her hips higher, finding that perfect spot where each thrust of Emry's fingers made her eyes roll back.

"Faster," she whispered.

Her words unleashed Emry, and her thrusting fingers picked up speed as her thumb dropped to Heather's aching button. The contact sent Heather crashing over the edge of her release, a sharp moan echoing across the cave as she shattered. The sound broke Emry, her climax roaring through her and their staccato breaths converging as their bodies released. They stroked each other through each wave of pleasure, their movements slowing further with each panting breath until they finally stopped.

"I always dreamt about coming here with someone." Emry's lips pulled into a smile against Heather's. "If only I could go back in time and tell myself it would be with the most gorgeous witch in all of Okrith. I don't think I would've believed me." Emry's hand swept up Heather's chest to her cheek, her eyes glowing a brilliant crimson.

Heather grinned. "I want you to show me everything, all the places you dreamed of sharing with someone."

"I want to share my whole life with you, Heather," Emry murmured, her fingers tracing up and down her back. "Every single heartbeat."

Emotion choked her words as Heather said, "I want that too."

CHAPTER TWELVE

Two weeks later

Clouds hung thick in the air, the humidity growing with each hour. Emry seemed immune to it—the line of sweat around her neckline the only indication that it was warmer than usual. Soon, the heavy rain clouds would relent to the cooler days of winter, or, at least, that's what Emry promised. But Heather wasn't sure what constituted as "cold" as they edged across the border into the Southern Court.

Emry manned their stall while Heather sat under the wagon window, where a thin sliver of shade provided some relief from the heat. She read a foraging book that she'd borrowed from the other brown witches. She'd yet to find anything specific to the Southern Court, and she hoped to find some use for the tropical plants in the surrounding forests. Ravi had gone inside the wagon, the raven escaping from the heat and occasionally poking his head out to make sure nothing exciting was happening.

A shadow fell across Heather's bare feet, and she looked up to see Emry standing over her.

"What are you looking at?" Heather teased as she squinted up at Emry's backlit face.

"Nothing." Emry shrugged. "You're just very cute when you're reading."

Heather's cheeks flushed, tucking one of her family's letters in the enormous book to keep her place.

"Do you have any witches' wort?" an elderly man called from across the way.

Emry turned back to the stall, readying to help him. Heather set her book aside, knowing she should probably assist since witches' wort, if misused, could exacerbate a malady rather than cure it. She could read the rest of these books in the evening once they closed up for the night. Standing, she grabbed her amber-brown apron from the hook above her and tied it on. She slid her feet back into her linen shoes, a sharp piece of straw pricking her big toe. She pulled her foot back to extract the splinter but instead found a large black scorpion scuttling out of her shoe.

She jolted backward; the scream dying on her lips. The chittering creature disappeared under the wagon and Heather stared down at the bead of blood on her toe. Fiery pain bloomed from that pinprick. Her skin started instantly swelling until the thin lines of her toe joints disappeared into her ballooning flesh.

"Heather?" Emry's voice sounded underwater as Heather clenched her teeth against the burning pain. "What's wrong?"

Her heart raced in her ears as she gritted out, "Scorpion."

"Shit." Emry dropped to her knees, pulling Heather onto her lap. She held up her foot, and Heather winced at the movement. "What did this scorpion look like?"

She indicated with her hands the size. "It was this long and black with giant claws," she groaned, panting as waves of pain rolled through her. Each breath seemed to make the wound burn as if she'd placed her foot into a fire.

"Good."

"Good?!" Heather exclaimed, dropping her head back onto Emry's shoulder and grabbing her neck. Her fingernails dug into Emry's skin as she tried to breathe away the pain.

"They're less venomous," Emry said through gritted teeth. Heather tried to ease the pressure of her fingertips, but couldn't. Emry dropped her forehead into Heather's neck, the contact of her warm skin easing her panic. "It won't kill you."

"Why doesn't that make me feel any better?" Heather growled.

"Breathe," Emry whispered in her ear. The tickle of her mouth on the shell of her ear made gooseflesh rise on Heather's arm. "The deeper you breathe, the more the pain will lessen."

"I can't."

"The venom makes your heart race," Emry said, placing her palm over Heather's forehead. "Your muscles tense and makes it hurt more."

"I can't help it." Heather balled her fists. She could no sooner relax than she could sprout wings and fly.

"It will pass soon, love. Try to cast your mind to something else," Emry murmured.

"You try doing that when your entire body is on fire!"

Emry swept a strand of Heather's hair off her face, dipping her head so that her storming brown eyes met Heather's. "Do you trust me?"

"Yes," Heather snapped, her voice sounding harsher than her words.

"Mallor!" Emry called to Ean. The blue witch peeked over

his table at them, the feather in his cap waving in the breeze. "Scorpion sting. Cover for us for the next little while?"

He gave a little wave and Emry's arms shifted around Heather, hoisting her up in her arms.

"Gods, you're strong," Heather said, burying her face under Emry's chin.

Emry chuckled, releasing her arms. Heather tightened her grip around Emry's neck, ready to fall, but she didn't. She floated in the air, Emry's red magic keeping her aloft. The red witch's powers kept her floating there as Emry opened the wagon door.

"That's so much cooler than healing potions," Heather grumbled.

Emry grinned. "Feeling better already, I see?"

"Hardly." Heather groaned, her whole foot now swollen and bright red. "Look at this!"

"The swelling will go down if you relax," Emry said, taking the steps up into the belly of the wagon two at a time. She carried Heather down the narrow corridor and laid her down on the patchwork couch.

"And how exactly am I meant to rela—"

Heather's words died on her lips as Emry reached back and yanked off her tunic.

"I have a few ideas," Emry said, sliding Heather's skirt up her thighs.

"You can't be serious." Heather's eyes widened.

The cushions bowed under Emry's weight as she placed her elbow beside Heather's hip. She hooked her thumbs into Heather's underwear and cocked her eyebrow. "Do you want me to stop?"

"I . . . No, but—" Heather couldn't finish the thought before Emry slid her underwear off, dropping the fabric onto the floor without taking her eyes off of Heather. Emry's stare flickered red, the magic flames in her eyes revealing her desire. Her rough fingertips skimmed across Heather's flesh as she pushed her skirt up around her waist.

Heat pooled in Heather's core, that instant tugging low in her belly replacing the burning in her foot. Her heart still boomed against her sternum, but anticipation replaced her panic as Emry's hand hooked under her knee and spread her wider.

Heather's lips parted, her eyes holding Emry's crimson gaze as she began to lower her head. Emry's warm breath tickled the hairs between her legs, and Heather knew she was so close to where she wanted her to be. A deep moan pulled from her lungs at the first sweep of Emry's tongue. Those slow circles set her on fire, the kind of wanton burning that superseded all others. Emry groaned against Heather's flesh, the vibrations sending tingles dancing all throughout her body.

In that moment, she didn't care if her foot fell off, so long as Emry didn't stop. Emry's fingers circled her entrance, teasing her once, twice, before dipping into her wet core. Heather's back arched as Emry filled her, massaging her inner folds up and down in rhythm with her tongue. Emry knew just how to move, the right pace of her tongue that zinged the most delicious pangs of pleasure throughout Heather's body. Her eyes rolled back as she gave in to the overwhelming sensation of Emry's tongue lashing over her throbbing clit.

Her moans grew more frantic as she clawed at the couch cushions, grabbing on for dear life as Emry's fingers moved faster. Emry pushed her higher and higher, making Heather's moans morph into breathless cries of pleasure. With one more lash of her tongue, Heather exploded, her muscles clenching over and over around Emry's pumping fingers.

When Heather's moans finally ebbed to panting deep breaths, Emry released her. She kissed her way up Heather's thigh and onto her belly, resting her hot cheek against Heather's skin.

"How's your foot feeling?" Emry whispered, and Heather could feel her grinning against the flesh of her stomach.

Heather swallowed, taking another few shallow breaths before she replied, "I think I need to go find a few more scorpions."

CHAPTER THIRTEEN

"How do they make a different breakfast every day of the week from the same rations?" Heather asked, leaning back against Emry's chest as she pulled apart the cinnamon bread.

"Magic," Emry murmured, kissing Heather's temple.

Licking the sugar off her fingers, Heather stared out at the turquoise water of Silver Sands harbor. They'd arrived the previous night well after dusk and Heather hadn't been able to take in the glorious sight until now. The light glittered off the metallic sand, making it shimmer like silver ore. The sight was otherworldly and breathtaking, as if Mother Moon created this magical place where her moonbeams glimmered even in the light of day. Choppy waves rolled into the harbor, but the caravan was sheltered from the wind, nestled between the trees.

The forests here were humid and lush, the greenery turning brighter and thicker as Heather stared across the harbor and into the jungles on the horizon. This was the first time Heather had ever left the Western Court—the thought thrilling and terrifying all at once.

"What's that?" Heather asked, pointing to a copper-domed building sitting proud atop the cliff. The circular structure was built of marble and robed figures walked the zig-zag paths down to the white stone house below.

"That's the archives," Emry said. "It's a brown witch library."

Heather's eyes lit up with recognition. "I've heard of it before, though I'd never thought I'd see it." She pointed across the harbor to a sprawling palace built into the rock. "And that?"

"The home of the Hemarr family." Emry's cheek pressed against Heather's ear as she grinned. "The fae family who own the mines in this region."

"I thought it was the palace," Heather murmured. "It looks fit for a King."

"Wait until you see Saxbridge," Emry taunted, wrapping her arms tighter around Heather.

The scuttle of leaves pulled their attention to the right, just in time to see the end of a black tail slither into the bushes.

Heather shrieked, leaping up and stumbling backward. "What in Moon's tits is that?!"

"You've been spending too much time with Ean," Emry said with a chuckle. "It's just a snake."

"Just?" Heather's eyes darted to the bush where the snake had disappeared. "It was longer than me!"

She scratched down her bare arms, suddenly feeling itchy all over. This part of the Western Court was crawling with all manner of creatures that seemed intent to bite and sting. Lizards the size of barn cats. Flying insects bigger than her fist.

"That was a Western king snake. They're harmless," Emry said. "They'd much rather flee from you than bite you."

"Good," Heather gritted out, dusting the sugar crumbs off her skirt.

"It's the ones with the red stripes that you need to look out for."

Heather scowled, crossing her arms. "I'm guessing your form of distraction won't work on that kind of venom?"

"No," Emry said with a foxlike grin, the memory of how she handled the scorpion sting making her eyes flash red. "Though I wouldn't be opposed to trying."

"How many other deadly creatures live in these forests?"

"A few," Emry hedged.

"And do you travel with remedies to these venoms?" When Emry shook her head, Heather's eyebrows lifted as if Emry had lost her mind. "What do you mean, no?"

"There's no antidotes that I'm aware of." Emry shrugged. "At least, the witches at the carnival don't have any."

"I'm supposed to be the brown witch healer for *Carnival du Fareas*." Heather frowned, crossing her arms. "I was never trained in snake venom antidotes. We didn't need them in Valtene. But, I'm certain there is such a potion somewhere. Some herb or plant must stop the toxins."

"I think I know who'd have the answer," Emry said with a casualness that made Heather frown.

"Where exactly?"

Emry pointed to the copper dome on the horizon. "If the librarians don't know, then no one does." Emry flourished her hand out to the path that snaked through the forest. "Shall we?"

Heather quirked her brow at the red witch. "What about the markets?"

"We can open up shop a couple of hours late," Emry said. "We'll get back before it gets busy."

This was the difference between working at a carnival and working at an apothecary. The apothecary business kept regular hours, rain or shine. The carnival made no such promises. One day they might open at first light, the other not until midday. Heather knew her sister, Rose, would hate it. She was always the one who was organized, who liked routines and plans. Opening their family apothecary even five minutes late would've irked her to no end. Heather still hadn't heard from her sister directly. She hoped Rose was doing well, enjoying her life running the family business like she'd always wanted to.

Heather moved carefully down the path, stepping through the dried leaves like a cat walking through wet grass.

"Okay, come on." Emry chuckled, crouching in front of Heather in a bid to get her to climb on her back. "We'll never make it at this pace."

"Pardon me for not wanting to be bitten by a venomous snake," she hissed, all the while wrapping her arms around Emry's neck. "*Especially* when there is no known antidote."

Emry's hands slid to Heather's thighs, and she hoisted Heather up onto her back. Heather's legs squeezed above Emry's hips as she took off down the trail toward the library. She walked as if Heather weighed nothing at all, and Heather was reminded once again of how strong this red witch was. She wondered how much of Emry's magic was holding her aloft, and, judging by the glorious bulge of Emry's arm muscles, she'd wager not much at all.

Her head bobbed as she lowered it to Emry's ear, timing it just right so that she could kiss her without their heads knocking.

"I love you," she whispered.

Emry grinned, fingertips pressing tighter on Heather's thighs. "I love you too."

CHAPTER FOURTEEN

The giant copper doors had faded to a shade of seafoam green, having been exposed to years of salty sea air. A brown witch swept the white marble stoop. Spotting them, her eyes dropped to their totem pouches, and she touched hers in greeting. She wore flowing cinnamon-brown robes, her silver hair braided back at the temples to keep her curls off her face.

"It's been weeks since we've had any visitors," she said with a soft smile. "Most stay away in the autumn. The weather is too unpredictable in these parts."

"That's why we're headed south to Saxbridge for the winter," Emry said.

The witch's eyes lit up. "Are you with the *Carnival du Fareas?*"

Emry grinned. "We are, indeed."

Heather smirked at the surprise in the witch's eyes. She was a part of this now—one of those carnival witches that seemed to light everyone up whenever they were near. Only weeks ago, the mystical witch carnival made her buzz with the same delight, and now she got to be one inspiring such glee in others.

"What brings you to our library?" the witch asked. "Come for this beautiful view, or are you looking for something in particular?"

Heather glanced over her shoulder out toward the glittering harbor. She understood now why people made pilgrimages to this place, why they'd break on the road southward to hike up these cliffs. This stunning vista felt like a waking dream.

"We're looking for books on snake venom antidotes," Emry said, glancing at Heather. "The carnival healer would like to have some on hand should we need them."

"Very wise," the witch said with a bob of her chin. She turned, and they followed her inside. "Though we have far more books on poisonous plants than venomous snakes . . . There are plenty of books at the brown witch temple in Swifthill on such things, next time you're headed that way, but I know the carnival moves south for the winter. Come."

They followed the witch as she navigated down the stacks of books. Heather craned her neck upward to stare at the shining copper roof high above them. Staircases spiraled on either side up to hidden levels above, and the bottom floor was filled wall-to-wall with shelves.

A few other witches watched from where they worked, giving Emry and Heather curious glances as they passed. A young witch with golden hair popped her head up from an opening in the shelf.

"Emry?" she asked, disappearing behind the stack and reappearing down their narrow aisle.

She was beautiful, with pale blue eyes, rosy cheeks, and a freckled nose. She looked a few years older than Heather. The witch walked straight up to Emry and wrapped her in a tight hug . . . one that lingered. The sight of it made Heather fidget with her hands, but fortunately Emry pulled away quickly.

"Marin, this is Heather. Heather, Marin," Emry said, making quick introductions.

The blonde looked Heather up and down, a fake smile making her cheeks dimple. "Are you the latest witch to be lured into the carnival by Emry?"

Her voice was high and reedy. She arched her slender brow at Heather, and the implication of her question made Heather's stomach drop. How many witches had Emry *traveled* with? Heather had never considered whether she had been the first. Of course Emry, gorgeous and oozing with charisma, had other lovers, but how many? Was the life they now shared just another on an unending list of escapades? Was Heather just on the ride for this spin around Okrith? Emry had told her that she wanted to spend the rest of their lives together, but this smug little witch was making her doubt everything. Heather tried to not let the feelings show on her expression as she pasted a pleasant smile on her face.

"Heather Doledir. I'm a brown witch healer," she said, not letting Marin define what she was and wasn't. "I'm selling my wares in Saxbridge over winter."

She didn't look at Emry. Let her think what she'd like. Marin needed to know that Heather wasn't just some weak little witchling riding Emry's coattails. She had her own name, her own purpose in life, and she wouldn't let Marin reduce her to Emry's latest fling.

"Splendid," Marin said with a grin that didn't reach her eyes. She turned back to Emry, her hand stroking slowly down her arm as she said, "Do come visit for a bit longer next time."

Emry stepped out of Marin's touch and nodded politely, the action making Heather feel a little less unsteady. Still, questions stormed through her mind.

"Let's see," the witch in front of them mused, wandering down the aisle and scanning the spines of books. "Ah, perfect."

She selected out a midnight-blue tome with golden lettering across the cover: *Poisonous Plants and Animals of Okrith, Volume II.*

"Where is volume I?" Heather asked, taking the book from the witch and flipping it over in her hand.

"Who knows?" The witch shrugged. "We are collectors of forgotten books. The ones of most importance end up in fine fae homes or witch temples." She dropped three more books into Heather's arms. "These should do."

"Do you have any ink and parchment?" Heather asked, eyeing the massive books. "I doubt I'll be able to commit all this to memory."

"Take them," Marin said with a wave of her hand.

Heather blinked at her. "What?"

"You can return them on your next turn around Okrith," she said with a smile. "We'll lend them to you for one year's time. I'll make a note of it in my ledger."

"Th-thank you," Heather murmured, gaping down at the precious tomes in her grip.

Emry took the top two books from Heather's hands, sharing the load. Heather didn't look in Emry's direction, though, still angry about Marin's comment.

"We'll see you in a year, then," Emry said with a laugh, seemingly not noticing Heather's change in mood.

"Be seeing you," Marin said in a saccharine little singsong as they walked out the front doors.

The elderly witch also lifted a hand in farewell, and Heather turned and left without waiting for Emry. She hurried down the steep trails and back to the main road that led to the fairgrounds at double the pace, scowling all the way. She had a sticky, dark feeling that roiled in her gut. The smile on that blonde witch's face, her lingering eyes and touches. The thought of her being with Emry, kissing her, under her, knowing how it felt to come undone with her hands and mouth—white-hot rage thrummed in her veins along with an equal dose of shame. She knew she shouldn't be jealous, but neither could she deny the feelings that swarmed her senses, overriding her logic.

"Heather," Emry said, hustling to keep up. "Talk to me."

"There's nothing to say."

"That's not true." In two long strides, Emry darted in front of her, forcing Heather to skid to a halt. "Talk to me."

"You and Marin," Heather asked, staring down at her feet. "You were together?"

"Yes." Emry's fingers found Heather's chin and lifted until Heather was forced to meet her flickering crimson gaze. She loved when Emry's eyes flared that brilliant red. She knew it meant Emry felt every bit as much as she did. "Do you worry I still have feelings for her?"

Heather's mouth dropped open at her bluntness, but no words came out. Of course, Emry would've had other lovers before her. She didn't know why she'd think otherwise, but . . . for Heather, there'd only ever been Emry.

She closed her eyes and took a breath. "How many were there?"

"A few. None lasted very long. Only a couple of moons at the longest." Emry's finger left her chin, sliding to cup her cheek as she whispered, "Look at me. Please."

Heather obeyed, watching the red flames dancing in Emry's eyes. "And this? Will this last only a couple of moons?"

"No." Those crimson eyes bracketed with pain at her words. She dropped her gaze to Heather's mouth and Emry leaned in, brushing a soft kiss to Heather's lips. "It scares me how quickly I knew it, but you eclipsed every uncertainty. The first moment I saw you, I think deep down I knew."

"Knew what?"

"There will never be anyone else, Heather," Emry whispered. "The sun rises and sets with you."

Emry threaded her fingers into Heather's hair, pulling her in with a soft moan as her lips enveloped Heather's. Her other hand skated down to the small of Heather's back, pulling her tighter until there was no distance between them.

"No one else." Heather felt the words deeper than any vow. "The sun rises and sets with you, Emry."

CHAPTER FIFTEEN

The pale winter sun rose above the trees and filtered into the wagon window. Even one moon from the shortest day, Saxbridge only had the slightest morning chill. Nothing a blanket and Emry's warm body beside her couldn't fix.

Of all the places they'd traveled, Saxbridge was Heather's favorite—the bright colors, the tastes, the scents carried on the balmy air. It was paradise. On every corner was a celebration, even in the depths of winter. The people were friendly and welcoming. Even the fae—of which Heather was now very accustomed—didn't turn their noses up at the witches. She'd had many nights drinking and dancing with some of the highest-born fae in the Southern Court and they treated her like an old friend. She knew then for certain she never wanted to spend a winter in the snow again.

A knock sounded on the wagon wall.

Groaning, Emry rubbed her eyes and barked out, "What?"

"Letter for Heather!" Ean called.

Heather bolted up, rolling out of the lofted bed and scrambling down the ladder. She was halfway to the wagon window when she realized she was wearing nothing but a lacy slip.

Emry chuckled as she remembered herself and Heather snagged a robe off the hook. Quickly thrusting her arms through the thick fabric, she cinched the waist and threw open the window.

"You don't have to turn your back," Heather snapped when she found Ean pointedly averting his eyes and holding up a letter behind his head.

He shrugged, peeking over his shoulder. "My visions suggested otherwise."

"You *Saw* what I'm wearing under this robe?" Heather asked incredulously as she plucked the letter from his grip.

He gave her a mischievous wink. "I can't help what I See."

"Yes, but I bet you can help how long you *linger* on that vision." She scowled and then her heart sank as she looked at the writing on the letter. Her playful taunting ended the moment she spotted Rose's handwriting.

"See you at lunch," Ean said, bowing his head and quickly excusing himself, and Heather could tell from his solemn tone that he already Seen the contents of the letter.

Her limbs felt impossibly light, an ache building in the center of her chest, and she knew without even looking that he was gone.

It had been weeks since she'd received a letter from any of her family. The last letter, which was from her mother, still haunted her. The words were pleading that Heather return before she never got another chance. Her mother's frantic tone had broken Heather's heart. But she'd said her goodbyes to her father, and he knew they'd be their last. Heather would've never made it in time. Her mother had seemed to accept that this was what would happen . . . until her father's health took a sudden turn and she panicked, wanting Heather to return at once.

And now, in Heather's hands, was her first letter ever from Rose—Rose, the stoic, steadfast sister—the one who would pick everyone else up and put together the pieces. She'd always been a little cold, but she kept order, kept people moving when they wanted to break.

Heather's fingers traced the perfectly curving letters, her sister's sharp attitude evident even in her writing. She drifted to the cushioned bench and sat, carefully opening the letter but already suspecting she knew what it said. It didn't stop the tears from falling when she read the first line:

Heather,

Father died two days after the last full moon. He was laid to rest in the family plot. Mother received your letter saying you could not return in time to say goodbye and I'm sure you made no effort to, not when you could have fun in Saxbridge.

Mother, in her grief, has appointed me owner of the apothecary and head of the family—a role you could have claimed if you were here. Seeing as you have no desire to be a part of this family any longer, this will be the last letter you receive from us. I will protect this family where you have failed.

Don't think of returning to Valtene on your next turn around Okrith. None of us wish to see you.

Rose Doldedir

Doledir Apothecary

The note crumpled in Heather's hand and she suddenly realized Emry was there, sitting beside her. Before the first voiceless sob could pull from her chest, Emry grabbed her, wrapping her up so tightly she thought she might crack a rib, and still it wasn't enough. She felt like she was free-falling off a cliff, nothing to grab onto, nothing to slow her fall.

Her father was gone . . . and now the rest of them too.

The thought blasted through her, hollowing out her heart. She'd never see any of them again. Her stomach roiled as she sobbed into Emry's shoulder. Emry didn't speak, didn't rub down her back, didn't move at all except tightening her arms at each pained gasp coming from Heather's broken soul.

Rose had twisted the rest of them against her. Did they all hate her now? Did they all truly feel as Rose felt? It wouldn't take long for them to believe it. A fresh wave of sorrow crested—she'd never see little Oliver again, never hear Evelyn's made-up tales, never listen to Cole's humming as he wrote in his journal . . .

Rose had taken them all from her, and her mother had allowed it. The family was probably crumpling right now, and Rose was the only pillar holding the whole thing up. Heather should've been there, or at least she should've tried. If she'd grabbed the fastest horse and rode day and night . . . it still would've taken her a week, and the lag from when the letter arrived meant even more. She and her father had already said their goodbyes, and, when he was alive, he'd kept the rest of his children from hating Heather for her choices, but now . . .

Her head drooped further into Emry's shoulder, and Emry finally circled a soothing hand down her back.

"Breathe for me," she whispered, taking a steadying breath herself and then another. "Breathe."

Heather's breath came in ragged shudders as she tried to match Emry's even rhythm.

"We will survive this," Emry promised, making a new batch of tears fill Heather's eyes. Heather shook her head into Emry's tear-stained tunic, and Emry squeezed her tighter. "We will survive this together."

CHAPTER SIXTEEN

One moon later

Emry's lips skimmed the shell of her ear. "You look like a Goddess."

Heather's skin rippled from her warm words and she twirled, her satin red dress swishing around her hips. It hung from her slender shoulders by thin red straps, skimming her figure and flaring out just below her hips. She relished the feel of the satin against her skin—the finest dress she'd ever owned. They'd bought the clothes at a local clothier, especially for the Winter Solstice celebrations, and the whole city was decked out in their finest attire.

Emry looked equally dashing in a silver tunic with matching red brocade and fitted black trousers that hugged her muscled thighs. It took every ounce of Heather's willpower not to run her hands over that leather and drift up to the firm ass she knew hid below the hemline of Emry's tunic. Emry looked at Heather like she was a masterpiece, but it was Emry who was the true Goddess.

It was a time of rebirth, of new beginnings, and, after an entire moon cycle of crying, Heather was ready to feel reborn. They planned to stay up all night, partying and reveling in the city of debauchery until they welcomed the first new light. She'd survive the longest night, and with the new dawn, she'd be reminded once more that she could survive anything.

Emry seemed to know how much Heather needed this reprieve. She'd been mourning the loss of her family to the point where she couldn't work, couldn't eat, barely rising out of bed.

When Heather agreed to attend the Solstice festivities, Emry had seized it like a lifeline. And, as she led Heather by the hand plunging their way through the crowds of revelers, it felt like Emry was dragging her up from the roiling waves of sorrow.

The sun had only just set, and the parties were already well underway. Regardless of the hour, it seemed like somewhere in Saxbridge there was always a party, but on the Winter Solstice, the entire court celebrated at once. Streamers and paper lanterns crammed every window and stoop. People spilled from doorways holding drinks and smokes aloft as they danced and sang.

The throng was dressed in the most vibrant colors, a rainbow hue of brilliant marigolds, cerulean blues, and enchanting magentas. Bangles of gold dripped from their wrists, and they waved pennants of silver and forest green— the patron colors of the Southern Court.

"Where are we going?" Heather finally asked as Emry dragged her through the crowd.

"My favorite place in Saxbridge," Emry said, waggling her brows at Heather. "I've been saving a visit for the Solstice."

"What is this mysterious place you're taking me?"

Emry winked. "Nearly there."

"Em—"

They turned the corner, pushing through the last of the crowd and emptying out into a massive botanical garden. To the left, people crammed the white marble patio that led to the open-air markets. To the right, flickering lanterns circled a long reflection pool, the candlelight casting shadows on the lush foliage and exotic flowers.

Their footsteps morphed from smooth stone steps into crunching gravel as they wandered to the far end of the reflection pool. The perfumed air of night-blooming flowers swirled around them.

A green witch circled the fountain, holding a smoking bowl and whispering prayers. Emry stopped in front of the old woman and bowed, tugging on Heather's hand to do the same.

"Moon Blessings, Baba," Emry whispered.

"Moon Blessings, child," the green witch sang back.

Heather's eyes flared. *This* was Baba Usha, the High Priestess of the green witches? What was she doing in the center of the Solstice revels? The High Priestess looked far too advanced in her years to be in the center of such revelry. Heather figured a High Priestess would be in her temple, lighting candles and whispering somber prayers . . . But, from what she'd learned of Saxbridge, that sort of prudish prayers didn't really match the personality of the green witches she'd met here. A green witch was meant to be in the center of verdant gardens, surrounded by platters of delicious foods. It was strange to Heather, but it made sense to the south.

Baba Usha dipped her thumb into the bowl, lifting it covered in gold dust. Emry leaned forward, closing her eyes and letting the witch brush the gold dust over her closed lids one by one. Heather leaned in, and the elderly witch repeated the action, gently sweeping gold dust across her eyelids.

Usha lifted the smoking bundle of herbs from her bowl next and blew the smoke into Emry's face, coating her in its essence from head to toe. When she repeated the action to Heather, Heather felt an instant calm, the sweet floral smoke clinging to her skin and filling her lungs. Her tingling limbs felt light and warm, her mouth parted as if savoring the sensation.

Then Baba chuckled and Heather opened her eyes to find the witch watching her with a cock of her head. She lifted a weathered hand and cupped Heather's chin.

"Sorrows ahead and sorrows behind are not the sorrows of the here and now," she said, sweeping her gold-dusted thumb across Heather's cheek. "Permit yourself this moment." Her gaze slid to Emry and then back to Heather. "Make memories now that you can hold onto in darker times."

Heather opened her mouth to reply, but the High Priestess simply dropped her hands and said, "Enjoy, young ones," before walking away.

"What was that?" Heather whispered to Emry.

"Moon Blessings," Emry said with a devious grin.

"Not the smoke," Heather said. She was a brown witch after all. She knew all about the smokes made from the flowers that grew on the banks of the Crushwold River. The people of the Southern Court used the purple flowers in their revels, thinking the hallucinogenic drugs could bring them closer to the Gods. "Her cryptic words. What do they mean?"

"It's what Babas do." Emry shrugged. "They're always imbuing that wishy-washy stuff on people. Come on, let's get some food."

"There's food?" Heather perked up at the word. She could

faintly smell the cooking coming from somewhere, but the scent of aromatic flowers and incenses clinging to her hair overpowered it.

Emry squeezed her hand, leading her back to the balcony. "It's the Southern Court," she said. "You think the green witches would celebrate without food?"

Heather grinned. "Good point."

The balustrade was laden with copper trays stretching from one end of the white marble building to the other. There was every food imaginable—curries and pies, sweets and cakes, flatbreads and cheeses. Heather's mouth salivated, not knowing where to even begin. Something about that heady smoke made her suddenly ravenous.

Emry plucked two glasses off a tray and passed one to Heather. She took a sip of the sweet bubbling liquid and hummed.

"This is delicious," she said, taking another long swig.

Emry's hand found the crook of her arm. "Go easy with that stuff. It's meant for sipping." She chuckled, her eyes dropping to Heather's mouth as she licked her lips.

Music lifted in the air, and the crowd raced toward the finely groomed lawns to dance.

"Perfect timing," Heather said, looking at the platters of food that they'd no longer have to compete for.

They ambled down the long table, tasting the bite-sized morsels. Sweet, savory, buttery, spicy—the flavors lit up her tongue, and she licked her fingers, enjoying each perfect mouthful. She let out an indecent moan as she tasted a pastry twisted with sugared cinnamon.

Her eyes flew open at Emry's laugh, and she realized she'd been closing them, enraptured by the taste.

"This food is . . ."

"I know," Emry said, cheeks dimpling. "It's the smoke. It heightens every pleasure."

Heather's eyes darted to Emry's, finding them glowing with flickering red light. "*Every . . . pleasure?*"

Emry arched a brow, her crooked grin making Heather's toes curl. She grabbed the drink from Heather's hand and hastily set it aside.

Threading her fingers through Heather's, she said, "Let's go, you temptress," and tugged Heather into the night.

CHAPTER SEVENTEEN

They stumbled out onto the tiled rooftop, the sky a stretch of stars above their heads. Emry clumsily shut the window behind them, clutching Heather around the waist.

"This is my favorite view of Saxbridge," she murmured onto Heather's lips.

Her tongue snaked into Heather's mouth, and all thoughts drifted to the recesses of her mind.

"I'll look at it later," Heather said, yanking at Emry's belt buckle.

Emry snickered, shoving Heather back against the steeply sloping tiles. She slowly lowered on top of her, thighs straddling Heather's hips. Reaching behind her head, she hauled her tunic off and threw it down beside her. It slid halfway down the rooftop, halting just before dipping over the edge.

Emry lifted on her knees and bunched the satin of Heather's dress in her hands. She dragged the skirt up until it circled Heather's waist. Her fingers trailed along Heather's collarbone and dipped under the thin straps of her dress, slipping them off her shoulders until Heather's peaked nipples were exposed to the air.

Heather let out a wanton pant, threading her fingers through Emry's hair as she dipped her lips to the crook of Heather's neck. Nipping her teeth in a trail, Emry licked and kissed down to Heather's nipple and pulled it into her mouth. Heather groaned and bucked, her hips grinding up into Emry. The sensation was nothing like she'd felt before. The smoke and wine twisted her mind, making her entire body buzz, every cell homed into the pleasure Emry pulled from her.

With a laugh, Emry released her and trailed lower, over the bunched satin and down her belly. Her breath skated across the lace of Heather's panties, and her hot finger brushed across the wet fabric. That slightest taunting touch made Heather mewl a pleading sound, begging for more. Emry's breath brushed across her flesh as her fingers pulled the lace to the side and she lowered her mouth.

Lightning bolted through Heather's veins at the first sweep of her tongue. Ecstasy rocked through her, making her throw her head back as Emry's tongue circled her bundle of nerves. She hummed at the taste of her, and Heather felt the vibrations straight down to her toes.

"More," Heather panted, her words ending in a desperate gasp.

Emry's fingers squeezed her thigh, spreading her wider before trailing toward her flooded core. They dipped into her wet heat, filling her as Heather barked out a cry of pleasure. Emry's fingers massaged her inner folds, fingers rolling in and out at increasing speed. Her touch was masterful, the rhythms of her tongue and fingers perfectly tuned to Heather's every breath and moan. Her tongue moved faster, fingers pumping quicker, until Heather's hand bunched into a fist of tangled hair. Her hips lifted of their own volition, grinding into Emry's mouth, riding her fingers as she chased her pleasure over that cliff.

When she exploded, the entire world seemed to shatter, her body the only thing that existed as wave after wave of euphoric pleasure coursed through her. She didn't know the cries of desire, didn't know her own voice, lost in the deep waters of molten ecstasy until the storming pleasure finally ebbed.

Her cries morphed into pants, and she collapsed back onto the cool tiles. She was suddenly aware of the star-filled sky, the tiles biting into her back, the wetness trailing down her thighs, and the distant sounds of music and cheering. Her senses slowly returned, and Emry kissed her way up to Heather's belly.

Heather's hand reached down and pulled Emry up to her. Their lips met, and she tasted her release on Emry's tongue. A groan pulled from Emry's lungs as Heather licked into her mouth.

"Take your pants off," Heather commanded, and a growl escaped Emry's lips.

She quickly shucked her boots and unbuckled her belt. Tugging down her trousers and undershorts, she tossed them to the side and dropped back down. Heather's hands slid between her legs, cupping her ass as she pulled Emry closer until Emry was straddling her head.

Emry snarled, knowing exactly what Heather beckoned her to do, and she lowered herself until her core brushed across Heather's open mouth. As Heather licked Emry up and down, Emry threw her head back, her hands falling forward as she scrambled for something to grab onto. Her hips rolled, finding her own rhythm across Heather's tongue. Heather's fingers clenched Emry's ass, feasting on her wetness and circling her pulsing clit as Emry groaned again.

Her desire rose in a sudden peak, and Emry dropped to

her forearms, grinding hard and fast against Heather's mouth until a sharp moan pulled from her lungs, punctuated by a snarling gasp. Heather lashed her up and down with swift, long strokes as Emry's climax roared through her.

With a last panting breath, she rolled off of Heather and gathered her against her chest. Heather's head tucked into her shoulder, her fingers tracing Emry's soft skin as she listened to the slowing of her breaths.

Emry rested her temple against the top of Heather's head, and they stared up into the stars.

"A new sun wakes in the sky," Emry panted. "A new life. One I'm glad we're spending together."

Heather squeezed Emry tighter and hummed in agreement.

Baba Usha's words floated into her mind. She didn't know what sorrows lay ahead, but she'd hold onto this memory tightly enough that it would live within her forever.

CHAPTER EIGHTEEN

Twenty-three Years Later

Heather's pulse pounded against her eardrums as she strained to hear the footsteps coming from down the hall. Emry's arms wrapped around her tighter, and Heather trembled as the floorboard beneath her boot creaked. Would the witch hunters hear it? Would the tavern matron pay for harboring them? Heather had spent every day of the last year wondering if this was it—if the witch hunters would finally add another red witch to their tally.

Emry screwed her eyes shut, curling her fingers into Heather's dress until her magic hid beneath the fabric.

"Steady," Heather whispered into Emry's ear as she shuddered.

The sliver of light that peeked from the doorframe flickered as shadows moved down the hall. Heather's heart leapt into her throat as she spotted the outline of two fae. They wore muddied battle leathers and menacing curved swords on their belts. How many lives had those swords claimed? The tavern matron, Mrs. Vensley, hurried after them, huffing about something under her breath. She smoothed her hand down her apron as she scowled at the trail of dirt trekked across her carpet.

A gruff voice grumbled from down the hall, "If I catch you lying to me, Mrs. Vensley, I will be taking my bounty from this very establishment."

Heather bit her lips together to keep from gasping, tasting the copper tang of blood in her mouth.

Mrs. Vensley's tittering laugh carried down the hall. "And I'll remind you, *gentlemen*, that I am a businesswoman and harboring red witches doesn't make me any coin." Silence thickened the air. "But you know what does? Ale and the lovely ladies that tend my bar. You two look like you could use a bit of both, should you wish to reside here tonight and continue your search?"

The two fae laughed, booming and heartless.

"Aye," one said, clapping the other on the shoulder. "Let's go grab a drink before we continue the hunts."

They turned and headed back down the hall with Mrs. Vensley a pace after them. The matron paused before the first step down the stairs, then turned halfway. She didn't look directly toward the cupboard, but they knew she was speaking to them when she said, "Ten minutes."

That was all the time they had. Ten minutes. She'd be able to hold them off that long before they continued searching the place.

As the matron disappeared down the stairwell, Heather let out a quavering breath.

"Breathe," Emry whispered, just as she had countless times before. Turning Heather in her arms to face her, Emry wiped away the tear on her cheek and pulled her into a tight embrace. Her lips brushed against Heather's ear as she said, "Breathe for me."

"Only for you," Heather whispered back, her fingers digging tighter into Emry's clothes. "I only breathe for you."

It was the most comforting feeling in the entire world—the feeling of Emry's body against her own. Heather had grown so accustomed to it over the years, it became like an extension of her own body, and she was convinced that at some point in the last two decades, they'd become one soul. One look, one lift of a finger, one ragged sigh . . . she read Emry's body like a book, and she knew that the red witch was struggling to keep her feelings hidden.

They'd traveled to the very north of the Southern Court, where the jungles were thick and the villages few and far between. The Southerners seemed the most inclined to help hide the red witches—some turning a blind eye to their presence while others, like Mrs. Vensley, would feed and shelter them.

But it could all change in a heartbeat . . . and Mrs. Vensley's goodwill had now ended.

"Come on," Emry said, threading her fingers through Heather's.

With her free hand, she opened the door a sliver and peeked out into the vacant hall. They tiptoed out and up the stairs to their attic room. Emry insisted they always leave their bags packed, always ready to leave at a moment's notice. The days of fleeing had become more frequent over time as the witch hunters grew more rabid on their quest for red witch heads.

Heather's stomach turned sour as her shaking hands lifted her bag onto her shoulder. The glass vials of her tinctures and remedies clinked together, and she reminded herself once more that she needed to wrap them more thoroughly.

Emry peeked out the back window, stooping to not hit her head on the sloping roof. "We'll shimmy down the trellis," she whispered.

Heather's eyes flared as she whirled to the window. "It will not hold us!"

"Would you rather we traipse straight past a bar full of witch hunters?" Emry's eyebrows shot up. "Besides, the hedge will break our fall."

"Wonderful," Heather grumbled, making Emry smile. "We're not spring chickens anymore, you know. What about your knee?"

But Emry ignored that. In two strides, the red witch was in front of her, grabbing her and pulling her into a burning kiss. Her soft lips sent a thrill of delight down Heather's spine. Emry's warm mouth tasted of spiced tea and marmalade, and she wished they had more time to sate the building need within her. Emry always calmed her panic, always the anchor in her storms. She rooted her to the ground when she thought the gales of the past year would snap her in two.

"I love you," Heather whispered against Emry's lips.

"I love you too, my gorgeous wife." The red witch's cheeks dimpled into a mischievous smile. "Now let's go jump out a window."

CHAPTER NINETEEN

The jungle teemed with life, the thick humid air hard to breathe. Heather swatted at the clouds of buzzing insects as they trudged through the undergrowth. Everything in this place seemed intent to bite or sting her. Welts covered her skin from the poisonous bark of the tree she rested her hand on, and relentlessly itchy bites covered every inch of her exposed skin. Once they made it to shelter, she'd use her remedies to heal the wounds . . . but soon they'd run out and they didn't stop in any village long enough to make more. If the witch hunters didn't get them, this jungle would.

"There," Emry panted, sheathing her short sword into its scabbard. She pulled back the last of the crisscrossing vines to reveal a dilapidated hunting cabin. "Just like that innkeeper said. We can shelter there for the night."

Emry took a step into the clearing when an arrow whizzed past her and embedded into the tree bark beside her head. They gasped, staring at the crimson fletching of the arrow protruding from the tree.

"Who goes there?" a scratchy voice called from the open

window. A hood covered the archer's face down to the tip of their nose.

Emry held up her hands in surrender and took another step out into the clearing.

"What are you doing?" Heather hissed from the safety of the forest's edge.

Emry tipped her head to the arrow. "*That* is not a fae weapon."

She took another step through the knee-high grasses, and the hooded figure gasped.

"Emry?" they exclaimed, yanking back their hood to reveal a long silver braid, warm brown skin, and glowing red eyes.

"Elena!" Emry called, racing to the threshold of the door.

Heather's stomach clenched, watching as the older witch rushed to the door and yanked Emry into a tight hug.

A sob escaped her lips as she held her. "I thought I'd lost you."

Emry held her just as tightly, burying her head into the witch's cloak. Heather clung to the edge of the clearing, watching as three more curious heads peeked out the windows.

Finally, Emry released the witch and turned back, beckoning Heather over.

"Elena, this is Heather, my wife," Emry said. "Heather, this is my cousin, Elena."

Heather dropped into a curtsy, but the elderly red witch stopped her and pulled her into a hug. She embraced Elena, wishing in so many ways it was her own family she was holding. Heather didn't even know if her mother was still alive . . . nor any of her siblings. Right after the Siege of Yexshire, the Northern armies began pushing over the borders, testing the resolve of the other Courts. She didn't know if she had any family left. All of Okrith was in chaos.

Elena released her and beckoned them both inside, scanning the forest again before shutting the door.

"What are you doing here?" Elena asked.

"The same thing as you, I presume," Emry replied. "Are you headed northward into the mountains? I hear there are red witches gathering there."

"No." Elena shook her head. "To the Western Court. The raincloud that clings to the mountains there is said to be too miserable weather for fae. We're hoping none will pass through those parts."

The rest of the group circled around them as they spoke. Emry seemed to know the other three adult witches in the group, giving them all swift hugs. A fifth person made up their retinue—a young witchling in a red cloak, whose head barely reached Heather's hip.

Taking Heather by the crook of her arm, Emry made their introductions.

"Heather, these are witches from my coven. This is Fallon, Sarah, Rhianne, and . . ." She turned to the witchling and quirked her brow. "Is this one of your daughters?"

The middle witch, Sarah, stepped forward a little too quickly, but Heather excused it as nerves. She couldn't imagine how harrowing the last year had been fleeing from witch hunters with a witchling in tow.

Sarah rested her hand on the little girl's shoulder. "Mine," she said, her eyes looking everywhere but at them.

There wasn't much of a familial resemblance, and Heather wondered if the girl took after her father. She had curly, midnight hair, brown skin that freckled across her nose, and a soft chubby-cheeked face. Her fingers danced a scarlet red, the first signs of her burgeoning witch magic—so young to already be manifesting her powers so brilliantly.

The little girl kept her eyes downcast and Heather wondered what horrors she must've seen. The echoes of trauma danced across the little girl's face, and it made Heather ache to see it. Heather crouched before her and extended out a hand.

"I'm Heather," she said softly, and the little girl lifted her eyes. They were beautiful, saucer-like eyes—brown flecked in emerald.

The little girl hesitated for a moment, just staring at Heather's outstretched hand. Heather's gaze softened, and she moved to drop her hand when the little girl tentatively extended hers out and said, "I'm Remy."

CHAPTER TWENTY

Heather awoke to the sound of a scream. The other witches roused from their slumber with a start, and Heather darted looks between them, noting Sarah was missing. Emry leapt to her feet, grabbing her sword as she stared out the window.

"Shit," she cursed, throwing out her red witch magic. In a blast, every window and door slammed shut. "Witch hunters. They've got Sarah."

Elena grabbed her bow and nocked an arrow, while Rhianne pushed Remy behind her.

A sword tapped against the door. "We know you're in there, witches," a booming voice called. "Come on out now, if you don't wish to meet the same fate as your friend."

Thick tears streamed down Fallon's face as her hands trembled. The sound of the taunting swords scraping against the wood made them all tremble.

Elena looked around the room and then down to the floor, stomping on a loose floorboard, the other end flying free. She tipped her head down to the earthen floor below.

"Crawl to the far end and run," she whispered. "I'll hold them off."

"Elena. No," Emry protested. "We can take them. I'll stay and fight with you."

Elena's eyes bracketed with pain as she looked past her cousin to Fallon. "You and Rhianne get Remy out of here." She looked back at Emry. "You need to take Heather and leave. Now. Protect the girl."

"Cousin, no—"

"You don't understand," Elena said, watching as they lowered Remy into the hole in the floor. She gave Rhianne one last nod, one final goodbye. The red witch's eyes flashed crimson as she nodded in response. "That girl is our salvation. We must protect her at all costs."

"The girl. Who is she?" Heather asked as the doors pounded again and Emry's eyes flared with magic, struggling to keep the door in place.

Elena's eyes flickered a matching red to her cousin's. "Remini Dammacus," she whispered and Heather gasped. "The last of the High Mountain royals and the only person standing between Hennen Vostemur and the Immortal Blade."

"She is just a child." Heather's voice cracked.

"Precisely," Elena said. "Which is why she needs our protection. She needs to stay hidden. Think of what King Vostemur would do if he could fell entire armies with that magical sword. All of Okrith would be doomed. Remini *must* live."

The shutters rattled and Emry screwed her eyes shut to keep them all in place as more fists pounded on the door.

"You must go with her," Elena pleaded. "She *must* survive."

Emry froze, torn between staying and fighting with her cousin, and running after the High Mountain Princess.

Finally, she released the shutters and pulled her cousin into one last tight hug.

"Go!" Elena said, shoving Emry away.

Emry jumped into the hole in the floor, helping Heather after her.

Elena took one red arrow from her quiver and passed it to Heather. "Give this to Remy. Tell her to stay hidden. Tell her to not give up."

Shouts rang out. "They're running into the forest!"

They scrambled under the belly of the cabin as Emry released her magical hold on the doors and the witch hunters came barreling in. The floorboards groaned above them and dust rained down as they crawled out the far side.

Screams echoed through the cabin along with the whizz of Elena's arrows, and Heather wondered if the witch might make it. Maybe between her red magic and those arrows, she would be able to defeat them.

When they emerged, dusty and covered in cobwebs, they spotted two fae witch hunters bolting into the forest, chasing after the others.

Emry stood, sprinting after them as she threw out her witch magic. Branches dropped in front of the witch hunters' faces, smacking into them as they tried to push onward.

Clutching his scratched face, one of the witch hunters spun and his eyes landed on Emry. "You," he seethed, staring at the red fire that circled her hands.

Eyes alight with greed and venom, he drew his sword, and Heather screamed. Sweat beaded on Emry's brow, her stare vacant, her magic already strained as she flicked her fingers and the sword scattered from the fae's grip. They'd been traveling for weeks on end, with no rest and barely a scrap of food. Emry's magic was as exhausted as she was.

The second witch hunter turned and drew his weapon as the first scrambled after his sword. Emry's magic was too weak to pry the second's weapon from him nor could she slow his steps as he came barreling after her.

"Heather, run!" Emry screamed, but Heather didn't move. Everything in this life, they faced head-on together.

As the witch hunter bowled Emry over, Heather leapt onto his back, taking the arrow from Elena and stabbing it into the witch hunter's neck. Blood poured down his tunic and oozed through her fingers as he choked and spluttered.

The second fae rounded on them, lifting his reclaimed sword. Heather braced for the killing blow just as another arrow flew from the cabin window and shot him straight through the throat. She looked up to see Elena's agonized face, blood trailing from the corner of her mouth. Her eyes gave one last flash of crimson before rolling back, and she collapsed below the sill.

Heather screamed again, shoving the dead witch hunter off of Emry and yanking her to her feet. Emry's eyes were glassy as she stumbled after Heather. Her footsteps faltered, and Heather ducked Emry's arm over her shoulder, practically carrying Emry through the forest. Every muscle barked in protest, but she wouldn't stop. She would heal their afflictions once they got to safety.

Heather's heartbeat roared in her ears, the other sounds far off as the remaining hunters shouted to each other, darting back into the forest in the opposite direction, probably circling back for their horses. Heather whimpered; there'd be no escaping them on horseback. She looked up at the vine-covered jungle . . . unless they were in a forest so dense their horses couldn't reach.

Hope flickered in her chest, guiding Emry away from the road. They stumbled through the thick foliage, Heather lifting Emry over rocks and ducking her under vines, deeper and deeper into the verdant heart of the jungle until they stumbled into a clearing with a giant old tree.

Its branches were gnarled, waxy green leaves reaching up toward the dappled sunlight like arms stretched in supplication. She led Emry over to the ancient tree and guided her down to rest against the trunk.

"Where are you injured, tell . . ."

Heather's heart stopped as she pulled away and found Emry's trembling hand pressing over a stick protruding from her gut.

"No, no, no," Heather chanted, examining the stick that impaled Emry straight through.

Emry's face was drawn, pained and hollow, blood pouring from her wound all the way down to her boot.

"I don't have my potions," Heather frantically whispered. "I'll double back. I'll get them and—"

"Heather." Emry's bloodied hand reached for Heather's face, cupping the back of her neck and pulling Heather's forehead to her own. "It's too late."

"No!" Heather sobbed. "I will not lose you. You are too strong for this, Emry, please. We will find a way. We always do."

"The girl . . . you have to find her, Heather." Emry licked her lips, summoning the will to speak as her eyes flickered closed. "Fallon and Rhianne won't be able to protect her. You are smart and cunning and—"

"No, please," Heather cried, her trembling hands pressing onto the bloody wound. "Stay with me."

"Promise me, you'll protect her," Emry whispered, eyes closing. "The sun rises and sets with her now."

Heather opened her mouth to protest, but Emry's body went limp in her grip and the world dropped out from under her.

CHAPTER TWENTY-ONE

The night was silent, not a single snap of sticks or chirp of crickets, as if the entire forest knew that death clung to this place. Heather sat there through the dark hours, holding Emry's lifeless body, feeling it grow cold, and a hollow emptiness settled in her as devoid of life as the now frozen forest around her.

Her keening sobs had morphed into utter emptiness, and she knew then that her life was over. Every flicker of hope now doused, every dream that Okrith would know peace again now dashed.

Heather would find the next nearest witch hunter and ram them through with her sword and they'd end her. That would be it. Take one last down with her, and then she'd go and be with Emry in the afterlife. Life had been stripped of sound and color and joy.

Heather dug into the soft, rich earth with her bare hands for hours and hours until they were bloody and raw. She lay Emry in that shallow grave, and it took her many more hours to push the dirt back over her wife's body. She sat beside that mound of turned earth until the sun rose, steeling her heart for her end of days. Tearing a strip of Emry's red cloak, she split it into three. She put two into her totem pouch and hung the other on the budding branches of the ancient tree.

Heather stared at that bloody red ribbon, flapping in the breeze—the only memorial there would be to the red witch she loved. Burning tears slid down her cheeks as the sun rose and she stared at the lone ribbon in the tree. She didn't want to leave this place. Maybe she'd stay here and stare at the leaves until the ravages of sorrow finally claimed her from this world. No, that would take too long. She'd make it quick, one last flare of vengeance. She might not be able to defeat Hennen Vostemur, but at least she'd take down one more of his pawns.

Marching westward, she filled herself with hate. She didn't care that her skin was marred by bites or that her weeping fingertips dripped blood in a trail behind her. She didn't feel the sting of nettles or the scrape of the branches. As she trudged in stalwart silence, Mother Moon filled her with a singular final wrath.

She made it to the trail, uncaring if she stumbled upon other travelers. Let them see her blood-soaked dress and dirt-stained hands. Let them know she had nothing else to lose, nothing at all . . .

Her foot paused, hovering in the air. That sound. Was it the whining buzz of insects in her ears? She'd become so numb to every sound and yet this one snagged her attention, rising above the din. She halted, listening.

There.

A soft whimper.

She shouldn't care, not in the slightest. The purpose of her life was buried beneath that tree . . . but, that soft heartbreaking sound made her stop. It was as if her soul existed outside her body, weeping somewhere in the woods. She spotted the peek of crimson cloak, hiding behind the trunk, and knew who it was instantly. Curse the Moon Goddess and her false promises, of course she led Heather here. A smile pulled on her lips as her eyes welled. Even after she was gone, Emry was still telling Heather what to do.

Heather took a tentative step forward. "Remy?" she asked softly.

The hooded child peeked from behind the trunk. Tears streaked her blood-stained cheeks.

"Are you hurt, child?" Heather wandered over, dropping into a crouch beside her. Remy held her hands to her chest, covered in welts from the poisonous bark trees. Heather reached for her hand. "I'm a brown witch. I can help you."

She looked around the forest, eyes landing on the whorled leaves of a berry bush. It wasn't exactly what she needed, but it would have to do. She plucked a leaf and rubbed it together in her palms until they were coated in vivid green. Taking a deep breath, she summoned from her well of magic and took Remy's hands into her own. She pushed her healing power into the plants, willing them to calm the sores. Breathing deeper, the sound streamed from her nostrils. Once, twice, three times. She looked down at Remy's hands, and the welts had notably reduced. They hadn't disappeared entirely, but the child could at least bend her fingers without grimacing.

Heather turned over her own hands, realizing the cuts on them had stopped bleeding as well.

"Mother moon," Heather whispered, knowing what the Goddess was trying to tell her. Though she couldn't bring herself to believe it, she heard the Moon's message as clear as the whispering candles on a Harvest Moon: *Through healing the girl, you will heal yourself.*

Heather infused that healing magic up Remy's arms. Each bout of her healing power healed her own cuts further too until both of them looked like their wounds had healed for weeks and not minutes.

"The others?" Heather asked, already afraid of the answer.

Remy shook her head, crinkling her nose as her beautiful big eyes welled. "I've seen so many people die."

Heather's heart cracked at that—to be so young, to have endured so much. Heather had seen such awful things in the last year, but she was grateful her childhood was small and warm and protected. It gave her the strength to endure it. That's what she wished for this child: a quiet life, protected, *loved*.

"I dare say they probably won't be the last," Heather said, her voice laced with regret. "But you can't give up. You must keep going." The words turned bitter coming from her mouth. How could she tell this child such things when she didn't believe them for herself?

"I don't know if I want to," Remy murmured, and tears began spilling down both of their cheeks. This child was a mirror to herself and Heather couldn't bear it. To have lost all hope at such a young age . . . the anger of it burned into Heather, branding her soul. She couldn't see a future for herself, but this child—*this Princess*—could have a glorious future if only she survived long enough to get to it.

"Have you ever been to the Western Court, Remy?" Heather asked, standing up and dusting off the front of her bloodied dress. Remy shook her head, nervously tugging on a curl of hair. "I think you'd like it—the waterfalls, the hot cider in the autumn, the blackberries in spring." Heather closed her eyes and took a deep breath as if she could taste it.

"Is that where you're heading?" Remy asked.

"I haven't decided yet." Heather's eyes softened at the girl. "It depends if you'd like to come with me."

Remy's eyes flared a brilliant shade of scarlet, and Heather's heart cracked, thinking of Emry.

"I'll only be a burden to you." Remy's bottom lip trembled as more tears poured down her cheeks. "I hurt everyone around me."

"You are important to this world, Remy, and I'm sure that can feel like an awful burden." Heather pushed a steady warmth into her voice, an even calm that Emry had so easily summoned. Heather was the anchor now. She was the deep roots in a tempest. "But I would gladly give my life for that hope, as would every witch who has fallen protecting you. One day, you will build a better world upon those sacrifices." Heather extended her hand to Remy, and the little girl stared at it. "One day . . . but first you need some warm food and some new clothes. We shall summon upon our strength for it together."

Remy took Heather's outstretched hand and stood. Her warm brown eyes branding themselves upon Heather's soul, and Heather knew in that moment she would abandon all of her plans for revenge.

This little girl. The Princess hiding as a red witch. The last person between hope and darkness looked up into Heather's eyes and asked, "Strength for what?"

A pained smile pulled on Heather's lips as her cheeks dimpled. One last tear trailed down her cheek as she took Remy's now-healed hand and turned toward the trail. "The strength to keep going."

~

I hope you enjoyed Heather's story! The journey continues in The Five Crowns of Okrith series! If you enjoyed reading this story, please consider leaving a review, sharing on social media, or telling a friend! -A.K. xx

PATREON

Join A. K. Mulford's Patreon to receive ARCs, book mail,
access to the Mountaineers discord server, spicy artwork,
and brand new stories!

ACKNOWLEDGMENTS

Thank you to all of my amazing patrons for making this novella possible! Your support means so much to me!

A very special thank you to my fae, royal, and goddess patrons: Audrey, Jaime, Kristie, Lauren, Linda, Marissa, Alyssa, Amy, Ciara, Crystal, Drea, Emily, Hannah, Kelly, Katie, Mandy, Latham, Sarah, Virginia, Leigh, Felicia, Mariah, Patricia, Stacy, Jessica, JeNaya, and Lauren.

Thank you to Sara Kingsley from Adore Editing!

Thank you to Holly Dunn designs for the Map of Okrith

ABOUT THE AUTHOR

A.K. Mulford is a bestselling fantasy author and former wildlife biologist who swapped rehabilitating monkeys for writing novels.

She/they are inspired to create diverse stories that transport readers to new realms, making them fall in love with fantasy for the first time, or, all over again.

She now lives in Australia with her husband and two young human primates, creating lovable fantasy characters and making ridiculous Tiktok videos.

www.akmulford.com

ALSO BY AK MULFORD

The Okrith Novellas

The Witch of Crimson Arrows

The Witch Apothecary

The Witchslayer

The Witching Trail

The Witch's Goodbye

The Five Crowns Of Okrith Series

The High Mountain Court

The Witches' Blade

The Rogue Crown

The Evergreen Heir

The Amethyst Kingdom

The Golden Court Series

A River of Golden Bones

A Sky of Emerald Stars